POINT—A Paratrooper's
Memoirs of Vietnam

Jack

As a fellow point man for the 173d you know all too well that—

Freedom Isn't Free!

Rick Butler

POINT—A
PARATROOPER'S
MEMOIRS OF VIETNAM

A Novel

Rick Butler

iUniverse, Inc.
New York Lincoln Shanghai

POINT—A Paratrooper's Memoirs of Vietnam

iUniverse books may be ordered through booksellers or by contacting:

iUniverse
2021 Pine Lake Road, Suite 100
Lincoln, NE 68512
www.iuniverse.com
1-800-Authors (1-800-288-4677)

Because of the dynamic nature of the Internet, any Web addresses
or links contained in this book may have changed
since publication and may no longer be valid.

This is a work of fiction. All of the characters, names, incidents, organizations,
and dialogue in this novel are either the products of the author's imagination
or are used fictitiously.

ISBN: 978-0-595-47521-6 (pbk)
ISBN: 978-0-595-91790-7 (ebk)

Printed in the United States of America

Point is so bad that 'dogs die and psychiatrists cry'—things that are not supposed to ever happen—not even in war.

PRELUDE

As a youth I grew up in northern Indiana—a small town named Griffith which was kind of sandwiched in between Hammond and Gary. I grew up in a blue collar family with my dad, Gene, working in the steel mills and my mother, Martha, worked as a hairdresser/beautician.

My immediate family had a military background as my Dad was in the Coast Guard (which became part of the Navy) during WWII. They did troop transports in convoys from Boston up through Greenland and Iceland to Europe. My Dad's service started right after Pearl Harbor and concluded at the end of WWII. My brother, Ken, joined the Navy after high school. He served in the Navy for 10 years including at least 2–3 years in Paris, France. My older sister Bev married her high-school sweetheart, Al who also served in the Navy. My younger sister, Bonnie was still in school when I went off to the Army.

As a kid, I did not have delusions of grandeur surrounding military careers or adventures. Mostly I was just a regular kid who learned to love basketball. Of course learning to love basketball in the state of Indiana was not an uncommon occurrence. The first basketball hoop I remember shooting at was nailed to a tree in our back yard on Wright Street. I remember shooting baskets with my brother, Ken and my Dad for hours on end. Maybe that's why I ended up being more of a shooter and playing forward as opposed to guard. Dribbling and ball handling skills were hard to come by playing on grass in a back yard as opposed to playing on pavement or cement.

The first organized sport I played was Little League baseball. It was here that I first met Marty who became my best friend. Marty was on another team in Little League but we were on the same team in Babe Ruth. He was a pitcher and I was a catcher—the fun we had and the stories we can tell.

The first organized basketball I participated in was a clinic (not unlike basketball camps today) in the fourth grade. The first team I played on was in 5th grade where we had try-outs and I made the team. I continued making the teams in 6th and 7th grade but somehow fell behind in 8th grade and was the last kid to be cut off the team. This was devastating for me but there were public basketball courts in the middle of our small town and I was determined to keep playing basketball. So I played basketball almost every day and almost always with Marty. In the dead of winter we would miss some days but I remember shoveling snow off the courts and trying unsuccessfully to bounce the 'dead' basketball but still being able to shoot.

I had decided not to try out for basketball my freshmen year because I didn't want to get cut again. But my Dad would hear none of that as he had played basketball for Griffith High and wanted me to play as well. He was convinced that all my play at the basketball courts had 'caught me up' and I would make the team. I remember he and I having a big argument over this and I went running out of the house crying. My Dad caught me and he said "if you don't want to try out for yourself—would you at least do it for me". He loved basketball and he knew I did as well. I told my Dad I would do it for him but I was still afraid I was going to get cut. Well, guess what? Father knew best. I not only made the team but I made the starting five on the 'A Team' and went on to play four years of high school basketball which was a highlight of my high school years to say the least. I was a starting forward for most of my senior year and Marty was our center. We had the best basketball team in the history of our school finishing with a record of 21–4 including our first ever sectional win in the state tournaments. In Indiana, back then, there were no tournament classes based on school sizes. We were a small school tucked in amongst the large Hammond and Gary schools so it was quite an achievement to win our sectional. Unfortunately we drew Gary Roosevelt in the Regional—a very big powerhouse basketball school. They beat us and went on to the state final championship game where they finally met their Waterloo.

In high school I had a 'B' average, mostly stayed out of trouble and was enrolled in a local college following high school. At the same time most of my friends and my girl friend, Judy, were going away to college. Marty received a basketball scholarship to Valdosta St. College in Georgia. No recruiters had talked to me about playing basketball in college so I kind of figured my basketball career was over. This did not leave me feeling very excited about gong to college to say the least. I remember one morning waking up and thinking—'I'll join the Army' and that will get me 'going away' too. Little did I know, this Army would not turn out not to be the Army with adventures that were portrayed so gloriously in the movies. Rather, this Army turned out to be the one that would take me to the jungles of Vietnam and all the horrors of war at the ripe old age of 18. (18—not old enough to vote or old enough to drink, but old enough to be drafted (or enlist) and fight in a war.)

Postscript: just after I had entered the Army and my brother-in-law, Al, the Navy, the first draft lottery was held. Al's birthday was picked #1 and mine #2 (out of 365 days). So even though we had both enlisted, our military service was predestined.

Authors Note: 'point' is a term used for the first position in an infantry formation during a combat maneuver. Think of it as the first person in a column of soldiers walking into harms way. Normally the point person proceeds alone for a specified distance (often 100 yards or so) and then if no enemy contact is made the rest of the fire team, squad, platoon and then company advances forward, in that order, linking up to the point man. The reason for this approach is to minimize chance of detection and casualties should the point man make contact with the enemy. Walking point is a very dangerous activity to say the least. Point men are very good, often crazy and too often end up dead.

This book is fiction but is based on my combat experience as a paratrooper with the 173d Airborne Brigade in Vietnam during 1968. Any similarity of characters or events in this book to real persons or happenings is purely coincidental and is not meant to injure, slander, incriminate or defame anyone. Some of the characters in this book are composites of two or more men who fought with me. The reason I am writing this book is because I'd like people to know what war is really about—in all of its horror. As an 18/19 year old, I walked point in Vietnam, a lot, and now I have post traumatic stress syndrome (PTSD). I probably would have PTSD even had I not walked point—but point made it big time. This book is dedicated to two great point men from the 173rd Airborne Brigade, Ray Garcia, and Mike Leech. Ray was the best point man I ever saw and he taught many of us how to walk point. I feel very guilty because out of the three of us, only I survived. I thought Ray and Mike were fearless and they probably thought the same of me. But the difference is I know I was scared and maybe that's why I am alive and probably why I feel so guilty.

Acknowledgements—a special thanks to the following people who without their support and help this book could not have been written. To my family Judy, Doug, Leslie and Maya thanks for listening to many of these stories over the years in a supportive way that has helped me with my PTSD which finally enabled me to write this book. They also read and gave me feedback and editorial support on many drafts of this book. A special thanks to Willie Prago (a Marine sniper in Vietnam) and Bob Wolfgang (a company commanding officer with the 173d in Vietnam), both of whom I volunteer with at the VA, for reading drafts of my book and giving me inspiration and support to continue. A special thanks to Gerry Stesiak (author of Raptor's Prey and a medic with the 173d in Vietnam) for his constructive editorial review and comments on one of my early (and naive) versions of this manuscript. Thanks to Ruth Sidhom (a fellow volunteer at the VA and a learned scholar on military history) for her review and feedback on this book. And last but certainly not least, a special thanks to Scott Smith—thanks bro, for your input on this book and most importantly for your bravery, sacrifice and service to our beloved country—Airborne!!!

C H A P T E R   1

▼

THE KID

I had just graduated from high school and was enrolled in a local college. Most of my friends were going away to school but my family could barely afford a local college. My girl friend, Judy, was going away to school and my best friend, Marty, had a basketball scholarship to a school in Georgia. So I felt I was being left behind and was unsure what to do about it. Then one morning I woke up and thought—'I'll join the Army'. I told my Dad, a WWII veteran, and my Dad was not happy as he had left school to join the service after Pearl Harbor and never returned to college. My Dad felt I was making the same mistake. But I didn't feel like I was making a mistake. I even decided I wanted to be a paratrooper. Exactly why, I didn't know—but the thought of jumping out of airplanes and combat seemed exciting—scary, but exciting. Surely this would be an adventure for an 18 year old kid.

I knew we were at war with Vietnam but I didn't really know much about it. I knew we were fighting North Vietnam and communism but that was about it. The draft was in effect in 1967 and the rules were if you went to college or got married, you weren't drafted. If you didn't go to college or you were not married you then were drafted and likely sent to Vietnam. Somehow these rules didn't seem right but they were what they were.

Army Training
Sept 67 to Mar 68

I went to basic training at Fort Leonardwood, Mo. Basic training is pretty much basic training. For some guys the physical demands of this training was a lot but not for this 18 year old basketball player who had also ran cross-country. In fact one part of the Army's P.T. test was a mile run in fatigues and combat boots. I always scored 100% in the mile run and was by far the fastest in our basic training company. My first sergeant talked to me about this because during an upcoming P.T. test we would be competing with the other three companies in our battalion. Our 1st sergeant made it very clear that he wanted me to win that mile run. But I was concerned because I heard there was one other guy in one of the other companies that was faster than me. I told Top (1st sergeant) that and he said he didn't care—he wanted me to win. Well the day of the big race came and the gun went off and me and this other guy took off. We absolutely left the other guys in the dust. Our pace was very fast—faster than I normally would have run but I kept up with this guy. A couple of times he tried to pull away from me but I was able to pick up my pace and match him each time. Towards the end of the race I was hurting but I kept pace until we got within 100 yards or so of the finish line. I didn't slow down but this guy had a kick left and I had nothing. He pulled away from me and beat me easily at the finish line. After crossing the finish line I threw up and all Top had to say was 'why did you let him beat you, Butler?' I said 'I had nothing left, Top'. And I thought that was pretty obvious as I was puking at the finish line. Top's response was 'I don't care what you had left—you shouldn't have let him beat you'. No credit for finishing second with a time of 5 minutes and 15 seconds in combat boots. But such was basic training. I had AIT (advanced individual training) at Fort Polk, La. Fort Polk had advanced infantry training at Tigerland where 95% of the graduates ended up with orders to Vietnam. Much of this training was specifically for jungle warfare to prepare us for Vietnam. All of this Army training was the first time I'd been away from home. I, like many others, were quite homesick. And I can tell you that the drill sergeants could have cared less. They were tough and very mean. I guess this was meant to harden you for the demands the Army would later make on you. But it was no fun for an 18 year old kid the first time away from home. At the end of AIT at Fort Polk, I got my orders for jump school at Fort Benning, Georgia, to be a paratrooper.... .

The first two weeks of jump school were mostly about physical training and mental abuse/harassment than about parachuting. They shaved your head again, like basic training. You had to run everywhere you went. They would get you up in the middle of the night, harass you, insult you and make you want to quit. We routinely went on 10 mile runs in combat boots and fatigues. The weak fell out or quit, the others got tough and persevered. They wanted you tough both physically and mentally for the demands that a combat paratrooper would face. In fact less than 50% of those who started jump school made it through and earned their jump wings

Some of the training was in fact about parachuting. I learned to do parachute landing falls (PLF's) where you are taught to land on the balls of your feet and to twist as you fall to go into a roll as you land. They also taught us how to jump out of the airplane after hooking up for a static line parachute jump. This is the easiest solo jump where you hook your parachute's jump chord to a cable within the aircraft. You hold on to your jump cord as you approach the door in single file to jump. Once by the door the jumpmaster says 'stand in the door' at which point you literally stand in the open door of the aircraft with your hands on the outside and wait for the jump master to yell 'go'. When ordered to jump you either jump or the jumpmaster will place his boot on your butt and shove you out. The reason you get kicked out is because the aircraft is only over the drop zone so long. So if someone freezes in the door for any length of time, others will miss the drop zone—possibly landing in trees, power-lines, etc. Overall, probably 95% jump, 3% freeze in the door and are pushed out and another 2% or so freeze up inside of the airplane and refuse to jump—thus terminating their jump status. If you wonder why 95% jump it's because we were brainwashed to take orders and we were proud to be 'airborne all the way'. We made our 5 'cherry jumps' during our 3d week of jump school, known as jump week. On our last jump it was very windy so to avoid being dragged by your chute after landing, there were quick releases you could engage to collapse your parachute. Something went wrong for one of our guys whose chute would not collapse and he was drug into a brick wall. His neck was broken and he was killed. So being a paratrooper was exciting and fun but also very dangerous. We completed our jumps, received our jump wings—and graduated.

The experience of parachute jumping is like nothing else. Once I jumped from the aircraft, my static line automatically pulled my chute open. After beginning my count to 5, I felt a tremendous jolt at about the count of three as my parachute opened. It felt as if my crotch was being pulled up to my throat as the speed of the aircraft and the prop blast from the propellers violently opened my chute. Once this happened I would look up to the beautiful sight of my white parachute contrasted against the blue sky. Immediately, there is dead silence. Even if there is a wind—I was blowing with it. It was as if I were deaf. But it is also peaceful and beautiful. Sometimes I could see clouds very close and sometimes I went through them even though I thought I could step off of them. I'd look down and see the ground. It looks kind of like a map. I had no sensation of falling but rather it seems as if the ground was coming up to me. When close to another paratrooper you can talk to them in a normal voice given the otherwise dead silence. And sometimes I came down right on another paratrooper's chute and I then simply walked right off it. It's kind of eerie and surreal—an unbelievable experience.

After jump school I had orders to go to the 173d Airborne Brigade in Vietnam. I had applied for O.C.S. (officer candidate school) but the Army said they had lost my application but I could apply after Vietnam. I had a 30 day leave during which I got engaged to my girl friend, Judy, with plans to marry after my year in Vietnam.

I couldn't believe it when my Dad (a WWII vet) told me he would take me to Canada if I wanted to go. He had bad feelings about this war even though he was actually on my draft board. When I told him I was going to join the Army he said he could fix it so I would never be drafted. I told him that no one did that for him and he went to WWII. I didn't think it was right that some kids who were fortunate enough to go to college got deferments, while others less fortunate got drafted and sent to Vietnam.

So, I bid my girl friend and family a tearful farewell. At that point I started realizing what I had gotten myself into and I started getting really scared.

CHAPTER 2

▼

WELCOME TO VIETNAM—LEARNING AND BEING SCARED TO DEATH

I never had read the Bible much but I sure did on my flight over to Vietnam. Somehow I thought this would help me be safe or get through the horrors that I was about to face. Now, in retrospect, I am thankful that I had no idea what those horrors would be. All I knew was that bad things were going to happen. I had no idea what they would be or how bad they could get. But I was about to find out.... .

Welcome to Vietnam
Apr 68

I'll never forget the blast furnace type of heat that hit us in the face as we got off the airplane in Cam Rahn Bay—welcome to Vietnam. Although the heat was unexpected, the fact that no-one was shooting at us as we got off the plane was a relief. We had no idea what to expect and as usual the Army hadn't given us a clue. As we processed in, we were issued helmets, jungle fatigues and jungle boots. These were lighter weight than normal Army issue and they were designed to be cooler and to dry out faster. I was already drenched in sweat so I guessed these would come in handy to keep us cooler and dryer with the heat and humidity. Little did I know that they were also designed to help us survive the Monsoon season (2 to 3 months of solid rain) which would come in November. After processing in at Cam Rahn Bay, it wasn't long before we got our military hops (C-130 flights) to our unit's base camp. Mine was the headquarters of the 173d Airborne Brigade in Ahn Khe. This was basically in the middle of Vietnam—the central highlands area. This area was characterized by jungle laden hills leading down to the rice paddies in the low lands by the South China Sea. We would soon learn that the enemy was in both areas—NVA (North Vietnamese Army) in the highlands/jungle and VC (Viet Cong) in the low lands/villages and rice paddies.

After processing in at Brigade headquarters, we processed into my company, A Company, 1st Battalion, 503d Infantry, 173d Airborne Brigade. The 173d Airborne Brigade consisted of four battalions . Each battalion had 4 companies and each company had four platoons. In our company the 1st platoon was called Lima, the second—Mike, the third—November and the fourth—Oscar or weapons platoon. Each platoon had three squads. Each squad had two fire-teams and a M60 machine gunner, an assistant gunner plus two ammo bearers (each ammo bearer carried their M16 plus hundreds of rounds of ammunition for the M60). A squad consisted of 12 men; a platoon had 3 squads plus a platoon leader and RTO (radio/telephone operator). In total a platoon had around 38 men and a company had 114 riflemen, 15 mortar men, 4 medics, a forward controller and RTO, a Captain as company commander and his two RTO's. A company at full compliment was 138 men. However we were seldom, if ever, at full compliment given casualties, etc. Normally we numbered somewhere between 80 and 100 men.

I was given my combat gear which consisted of a ruck sack (back pack), plastic poncho, a light weight camouflaged blanket called a poncho liner, 7 days worth of c-rations, 2 canteens and a canteen cup, a webbed ammo belt with suspenders, 4 hand grenades, 20 magazines (clips) of M16 ammunition with each clip containing 18 bullets, a claymore mine with a remote firing device, a LAW (hand held rocket launcher) and last but not least our M16—a fully automatic assault rifle. A M16 can shoot fully automatic, like a machine gun (1 clip lasts about 4 seconds) or you can conserve your ammunition by shooting semi automatic—single shot. Each c-ration box contained canned food (meat, fruit, crackers and peanut butter), a small pack of cigarettes, toilet paper and heat tablets similar to Sterno. All of this gear weighed 70 to 80 pounds. And little did I know but my M16 would be in my hands or at my side 24 hours a day for the next year.

After being overwhelmed by all of the gear/weapons we were given, we were told where the mess hall was and to eat and get a good night sleep in the barracks because tomorrow morning we were going out to the field to join our company. I did not get much sleep that night.

Combat Operations
Apr 68

The next day we put on all of our gear and struggled getting on the Huey helicopters that took us to our company. As we came down it was like we were landing in the jungle—not another base camp as I had envisioned. The jungle was unlike anything I had ever seen before. I later learned this was a triple canopy jungle. A canopy was a growth of trees with their branches and leaves spanning and creating shade. In a triple canopy you have three layers of tree-tops—each layer significantly higher than the previous one. The effect of this was shade being shaded by shade being shaded by shade. The end result of this was on a clear sunny day it was only twilight on the jungle floor making for an eerie, surreal affect. We landed in a small area that had been cut out and cleared in the jungle. We got off the helicopters and saw a few of our soldiers here and there but they were spread out in a perimeter where foxhole positions had been cut out of the jungle and dug out. They were reinforced with sandbags and tree trunks had been cut and laid on top of each foxhole for more protection. These seemed to be makeshift positions at best and the next morning I learned why as we abandoned them. But I'll never forget that first day and night. I was scared to death fearing I would be shot at any time. At night I was awoken for my 2 hour turn on guard duty. It was so dark I couldn't see anything and I tripped and fell into the foxhole as I was taking up my guard position. Once I was in place the other guy who had been on guard left and there I was, alone in the jungle, and not able to see a thing. Then I started to notice some of the vegetation on the jungle floor seemed to be kind of an iridescent green. That was all I could see and I had no idea what caused the iridescent glow but have since been told it was decaying vegetation. I strained to see if the enemy was sneaking up on us. It was a very long 2 hours—but I didn't have to worry about falling to sleep. Sleep doesn't come when you are scared nearly to death. I managed to survive my first night and the next morning we moved out through the jungle in single file, on our mission, as we walked and climbed our way through the jungle all day. In the late afternoon we formed another perimeter only to cut out and build new foxholes (sand bags, logs, etc) for the next night. After carrying my 70 plus pounds of gear all day and fearing enemy contact at any minute, I was exhausted when we finally stopped. But I then had to take my turn digging out the foxhole, filling sand bags and cutting trees to complete our fortified foxhole (known as a lagger site). I was never so tired in my life.

At the crack of dawn we were woke up and told to get ready to go. As I got up I saw a giant centipede whose body was about

4 inches in diameter and it was about a foot long. Someone grabbed a machete and hacked it into about 5 pieces, each of which scurried away in a different direction—welcome to the jungle and horrors of Vietnam.

I was surprised at the sounds of the jungle. I would have expected the monkey calls, etc that we all heard in the Tarzan movies. But that was not the case. The jungle was a mixture of sounds—mostly birds and other unidentified animals. Normally, however, the jungle was eerily silent. At night the jungle seemed to sleep. During the day we could hear the jungle wake up at dawn. But no sooner than we got up and started moving around the jungle went silent again. It was almost as if the jungle was afraid of us—the unwelcome intruders.

A few days later we were in the jungle near a stream and there was a lot of bamboo growing in the area. Someone warned us of 'two step snakes'. They were bamboo vipers and it was said that if you were bit by one you would take two steps and fall down dead. One of the guys in our squad was named Dooley. He was from Tennessee and was one of the good old boys who apparently were not afraid of snakes. Somehow he managed to catch a bamboo viper and was milking its venom on the side of a C-ration can. I couldn't believe it, but I soon learned that there were many things in the jungles of Vietnam that were unbelievable—but all too real.

They called us FNG's (f…. new guys). Although my unit had numerous recent casualties in the battles of Dak To, Ban-MeThout (the St. Valentine's Day Massacre) and Kontum (Rocket Ridge) and therefore needed replacements, there still was a stigma with new guys. They hadn't been in combat before and they easily screw up and screw ups in combat can lead to people being killed. Generally the reference to us as FNG's continued until our uniforms faded and we'd experienced our first fire fight. But there is no question, we (FNG's) were easy to spot with our new uniforms/gear and the 'on-guard/scared attitude' that we constantly displayed. This compared to the laid back more casual attitude of the combat veterans. No shirt, no helmet during lulls in the action within our perimeter was very common. But when enemy contact was made these warriors got dead serious and knew exactly what to do.

And speaking of Dak To, it was one of the biggest, most deadly battles the Army experienced in Vietnam. As a FNG I heard hushed talk about the battle—but mostly the survivors were in shock and didn't want to talk about it. I only learned later how bad it was and how lucky I was to have missed it by 5 months or so. BanMeThout and Kontum were only a month or two prior to my arrival.

As a new guy you were lucky if one of the grizzled veterans took a liking to you and took you under his wing to show you the ropes. I was lucky this way as Ray Garza took me under his wing-maybe because I was so young, 18 when I got to Vietnam. Garza would walk next to me in line as we moved through the jungles letting me know what was going on and what to do if something happened. I remember our first enemy contact, snipers, who opened up on us. With the first crack of the AK47 automatic weapon, Ray had us hit the dirt and crawl to cover. My heart was beating so fast and I was breathing so hard I thought I might die—but I didn't. The point platoon ultimately tried to flush out the snipers but they took off as was often the case—hit us and run.

It's funny how Vietnam brought guys together who otherwise would never have met. This was true of Ray and me. Ray was Hispanic and was from Albuquerque, New Mexico. I am

Caucasian and am from a little town between Gary and Hammond, Indiana. We were born and raised over a thousand miles from each other. When I got packages from home it was basically cookies. When Ray got packages from home it was hot stuff (peppers and other things unknown to me) and sometimes tequila with the worm inside. We shared it all including even the worm. Ray was kind of quiet like me but he loved to laugh and always had a smile on his face. He said he was from a large family with many brothers and sisters. It was rumored that Ray's family had been in New Mexico since the Spanish arrived in the 1700's. Ray was just a nice guy. He wasn't very tall, maybe 5'8" but Ray should never have been underestimated. When the 'shit would hit the fan' he was always there and he would fight like there was no tomorrow. If you ran into trouble—Ray was the guy you wanted with you. Ray almost seemed too nice to be in a war but make no mistake about it—this nice little guy who laughed and smiled all the time was a fierce warrior. There were times when some of the guys tried picking on me because I was a FNG. But with Ray there all he had to say was one word and they stopped. Ray, in spite of his small size and nice, quiet demeanor, commanded respect in a way I had never seen before or have never seen since. Ray was a point man extraordinaire and he was revered in almost a legendary manner.

Ray Garza and Rick Butler

First Combat Assault
Apr 68

Word came down to us that we were going on a C.A. A 'C.A.' is a helicopter combat assault using Huey helicopters. Each helicopter had a pilot, co-pilot and two door gunners with M60 machine guns on each of the two open sides. These Hueys had no doors so 4 to 6 of us could sit on the floor of the helicopter with our feet on the runners as we were flown into our combat assault. A pre-designated landing zone was chosen for each of these missions. If we were in the highlands/jungles then the landing zone would have to be a clearing. Often the clearings in the jungles were covered with a giant grass-like growth which we called 'elephant grass'. It was 4 to 10 feet high so the choppers would merely hover above the grass and we would jump out. Sometimes the landing zone was hot meaning we took enemy fire as we sat down but often as not they were cold L.Z.'s with no fire.

Almost always they would have gun ships which were Huey helicopters equipped with automatic 40 millimeter (MM) cannons and mini-guns that would strafe the LZ before our first chopper went in. The 40 MM guns were essentially like a machine gun that shot hand grenades whereas the mini-guns were extremely rapid fire M16 Gatling type guns. They say in one pass over a football field mini-guns could place an M16 round in literally every 3 square inches of the field. Usually if the LZ was hot, the enemy would return fire on the gun-ships attempting to shoot them down. So with radio communication from the gun-ships we were told if the LZ was hot as evidenced by the enemy fire directed at the gun-ships. Needless to say, hot LZ or not, the helicopters carrying us wanted to spend as little time as possible dropping us off. So they seldom would land but would briefly hover as we jumped off. If the LZ was hot the door gunners would be firing their M60 machine guns as they dropped us off.

My first C.A. was uneventful as the landing zone was not hot and we did not encounter the enemy as we deployed from the helicopters. This was not a disappointment for me. A C.A. without enemy contact was exciting enough. Sitting on the floor of a helicopter with your legs hanging out so your feet were on the struts and then jumping out of the chopper as it hovered 5 to 10 feet above the ground was a new experience to say the least. And of course you never knew for sure if the LZ would be hot or cold until you landed. So your heart would be pounding a mile a minute as your chopper came down to land. Our LZ was just outside the edge of the jungle.

Combat assault from a Huey Helicopter

It was late after we landed so we set up our perimeter for the night. I remember at dusk hearing a strange sound kind of like 'coo coo', 'coo coo'. This noise was from lizards which were 6 to 10 inches long. The GI's called them 'f.... you' lizards. About sunset we looked across a ridge and you could see what looked like mini dragons running. They looked to be about 6 feet tall. I couldn't believe my eves. I felt I must be a sleep, having a nightmare. But I wasn't having a nightmare—only experiencing another Vietnam terror. Back then we had no clue what those were but I think these were komodo dragons. Whatever they were, they reinforced the God-forsaken feelings we had about this place. There were smaller terrors as well in the jungle. Leeches were all over the jungle—not just in water. It was like they could smell you. You could see them raise up and kind of look around and then they would crawl toward you as if they could smell your blood. At one point I found a leech that had attached itself on the inside of my arm just down from my arm pit. It apparently had been there for some time as it was the size of a half dollar. I squirted it with insect repellent and it fell off but it must have been attached to a major blood vein as blood just poured out and kept running freely down my arm. I went to the medic and he had to put a tourniquet on my arm for about 10 minutes to get it to stop. I wondered how I managed to get myself into this God-forsaken place. But some guys put leeches to some good as they used them on their pussie jungle rot. The leeches apparently sucked out the puss and then fell off and died. To me this sounded like two wrongs trying to make a right. So I'm glad it wasn't done on me.

I was in great physical shape as an athlete just out of high school so basic training, AIT and jump school were physically tasking for most but not for me. However, the first time I went on an extended march in Vietnam (we called them humps) with my 70 pound rucksack in the tropical heat and humidity, it kicked my ass. We probably went 3 or 4 clicks (3 to four thousand meters—2 to 3 miles) and I can tell you I barely made it. Not only did you have the weight on your back you were often going up and down hills through the jungle. Although the point man would cut a path through the jungle it was often very tight with vines, etc grabbing you as you went through. The good thing about walking in a column with a point man, you had breaks as the point man would push forward, the rest of the column rested and then would link up.

Early in May of '68 we were assigned to bridge security along highway 19. We had a 'check-point at each bridge where we guarded the bridges against enemy attacks. Our squad was assigned to 'checkpoint 21'. Each checkpoint had a guard tower and at night we took turns on guard duty in the towers. During the days we routinely ran patrols out from the check points looking for enemy activity. And where there were GI's in areas assessable by civilians, there were whores. It's like the GI's were magnets and the whores were attracted. At one of the checkpoints, not far from us, the whores would routinely skinny dip with the GI's in the river which was good advertising for the business of whoring. Well, all was not fun and games at these check points as evidenced by what happened at check point 20. One night a group of V.C. snuck up on their position and hit them with satchel charges which were explosives carried inside a small case. One of our guys was killed and another had his foot blown off. It wasn't long after that we were reassigned back to combat operations in the jungle.

Bridge Security along Hwy 19

Happy Valley
June '68

Happy Valley was rumored to have gotten its name from the NVA who would smoke pot and laugh a lot in this area. But for us, it was anything but happy. This area was also known as Bao Loc. Our first time in Bao Loc we were CA'ed in to find a missing lieutenant. He had apparently been out on an ambush with one of his squads and the next morning he was gone. There had been no enemy contact but all that was left of the lieutenant was his helmet and rifle. No one had a clue what happened to him. This area was heavily jungle laden so he could have left the ambush site to go to the latrine and got lost but no one heard him yell. The general consensus is that somehow the enemy had snuck up on him and captured him without making a sound. But even this seemed unlikely. Anyway, we were sent in there to try to find him. Although it was not officially monsoon season, it rained as if it was. So we tramped around the jungle in the pouring rain looking for this lost lieutenant. At one point the rain eased up and a large group of giant hornets came upon us. These hornets were not just big—they were as big as cigars. A couple of guys got stung but no-one died or had to be medivaced (medically evacuated via helicopter). That's about all we found, giant hornets, but no lieutenant. He was (and still is as far as I know) listed as a POW/MIA.

We came back to Happy Valley a second time and we found an NVA hospital near Suoi Ca. Smitty and Dickson were on point along with Budha and Virgil—all seasoned combat veterans from one of the other squads in our (Mike) platoon. The hospital was in a well concealed, deep ravine between two ridgelines. As our point squad proceeded down the left ridgeline a large element of NVA had left leaving behind fresh footprints and laid down grass in an open and exposed area. It felt like an ambush so the point squad called the lieutenant and held their position until the other squad in our platoon could come down and cover their flank. Then Smitty and his point squad proceeded through the boulders and found all kinds of tunnels and rooms with medical equipment. Since Dickson was so small he volunteered to go down a tunnel and he pulled out a female nurse and then a male doctor. Dickson was awarded an in-country R&R at Vung Tau but he never made it. After Smitty and Dickson took the two POW's up to the command post Smitty took a machete and was cleaning up around his hooch and somehow managed to cut his leg. Our medic, Doc

Waters, said it was deep and could see a vein so he sent Smitty back to the battalion aid station for stitches. Two days later Smitty was scheduled to go to Australia on R&R but he never made it as he came down with malaria the night before his flight to Cam Rahn Bay.

First Time on Point
May 68

As I said, Ray Garza took me under his wing and showed me the ropes. The good news is Ray was very good. The bad news, if you can call it that, is Ray walked point and wanted to teach me. Ray and Smitty from the other squad in our platoon were our primary point men. Both had survived Dak To and were well seasoned in combat & point. I remember the first time Ray took me with him on point. It was on the job training. No traditional training class could ever come close to teaching you how to react and overcome the nearly unbearable fear. We were operating in the mountains/hills of the Central Highlands, in Vietnam's II Core. Mostly the terrain was characterized by dense jungle. I had a lot of trouble sleeping the night before walking point with Ray for the first time. At day break the word came down to get up, have some chow (C-rations) & get packed up because we were moving out. Ray and I moved quickly to get ready and then met with the platoon leader and platoon sergeant. They briefed us as to where we were headed and how to proceed. We were in the jungle but not the deepest triple canopy jungles we were in before and would soon encounter again. We had maps and compasses so we could navigate our way through the jungle. Mostly we would be clearing our own paths with machetes but we would also encounter some unexpected paths which likely had been cut and used by the NVA or VC.

Ray and I set out with Ray in the lead. He was hacking his way through the jungle, encountering vines, small trees, tall grass and the like. At times we could see through the foliage, up ahead a little way—maybe 10 to 20 yards. Other times we could see nothing but the dense jungle which we hacked our way through. Again, as point we would push forward 50 to 100 yards, depending on the denseness of the jungle. We would stop and listen for any sounds of the enemy and then proceed forward. We repeated that cycle until we had made enough progress for our fire-team to link up. At that point we would stop and wait for them to catch up. We would rest while the others were linking up. We would kneel down and then kind of flop over on our backs to get the weight of the rucksack off of you. I could then lean back and use my rucksack as a back rest as you sat on the jungle floor. As we waited for the link-ups we always faced out into the jungle—facing in alternate directions. One guy would be facing right, the next guy facing left, etc. This was done to provide security against enemy attacks from our flanks. This security was not flawless, however, as one time one of the guys we called 'water trailer' was shot while facing out from the trail in the deep jungle. (He was called 'water trailer' because he carried more water and canteens than anyone else.) After the fire-team linked up, the point squad, the point platoon and then the other platoons in the company would link up as well.

After our squad linked up to the point person (Ray and I in this case) we would push forward repeating this cycle. I remember clearly that first morning on point when Ray and I pushed off. It's one thing to walk behind other soldiers knowing they had not made contact with the enemy, but on point you are the man. Although I knew Ray was an extremely good point man, I also knew that even the best can walk into disaster. My heart was in my throat and was beating wildly as we pushed off for the first time. I was breathing very hard and wondered how I would make it for the 3500 meter distance we had planned for the day. But somehow I did. We always did. There was no stopping because we (our company) waited for no-one.

If someone got tired, hurt or scarred to the point they couldn't continue—their buddies would drag them along and sometimes carry them. There was nowhere else to go—we all had to continue. If someone got wounded/hurt real bad we might stop our march early if there was a reasonable clearing in the jungle for helicopters to land or one that we could clear for a landing zone. In that case we could call in a medivac (medical evacuation) helicopter to extract the wounded/hurt soldier and take them to a fire-support base/base camp for medical attention. But a medi-vac was a last resort option, only if our medics could not deal with the situation. Medi-vacs gave away our position to the enemy and sometimes the helicopters were shot down. So the decision for a medi-vac was only made by the CO. If someone was hurt and needed medical attention but not necessarily immediately, the other option would be for them to continue on if they could until it was time for us to be re-supplied.

Ray and I proceeded hacking our way through the jungle on point. From time to time Ray would stop & put his finger up to his mouth (indicating to be quiet) and he listened for any sounds of the enemy. The first time Ray did this I thought he had heard something but I learned that he had not but was only being cautious. After a while we came upon a bit of a clearing and there was a path to and from this clearing. The path extended in the basic direction we needed to go. So it seemed logical to take the path rather than to hack your way through the jungle. Ray told me that if we decided to take the path we would have to be extremely careful of booby-traps. Given the jungle was even denser in this area, Ray decided to take the path. As we approached the path, Ray proceeded with extreme caution and moved very slowly. He told me we were looking for signs of an enemy ambush, a trip wire or a pressure plate device. An ambush would be in the form of either VC or NVA hiding along the path—waiting to shoot us. A trip wire is a very fine wire that is nearly invisible. It is stretched across a path and hooked up to some type of explosive device. They are set up to be so sensitive that you would likely not even feel the wire if you tripped it. But even if you did feel the wire it would be too late. And lastly a pressure plate device would be buried in the path with some sort of camouflage over it—possibly leaves hooked up to some type of explosive device. This device is wired to the bobby-trapped explosive. So when you step on the pressure plate, the explosive device is detonated. Ray told me that sometimes the enemy would also set bobby-traps in the jungle on either side of a path. This was designed to catch 'smart point-men' who wanted to follow the path but were leery of bobby-traps on the path.

Ray and I proceeded on the path—moving ever so slowly looking for trip wires, hidden pressure plates and enemy soldiers lying in wait to ambush. Every step I took was nerve wracking for fear of being blown up or ambushed. It didn't take me long to understand the trade-offs of being able to move more quickly down a path versus hacking your way through the jungle. The other advantage of a path is that you can be very quiet as you proceed. Whereas being quiet was not an option as you hacked your way through the jungle. I started falling behind Ray again, because I was afraid to move too fast. Ray had me walk directly behind him and he picked up the pace while still being very careful as I followed. I watched the way Ray observed everything—up, down and to both sides. Every once in a while he would stop and kneel down—all the while looking intensely at his area of concern and then he would get up and proceed. All the while pushing forward and then having the rest link up—only for us to push forward again. We had followed the path for nearly an hour when Ray told me to go first. My heart thumped in my chest as the fear was nearly paralyzing but I managed to move forward—very slowly at first but faster with Ray's encouragement. I have never felt my senses so keenly aware of my surroundings. My eyes glanced this way and that—all the while straining to hear anything unusual while being extremely quiet. On point you have your M16 at the ready with the safety off and the rifle set to fully automatic (machine gun mode). When in this heightened state of awareness you suddenly start hearing and seeing things that previously seemed not to be there or a part of a general background of noise and sight. It's as if your senses become keenly sharpened in no other way you have ever experienced.

After a couple of hours on the path Ray checked his map and compass as we moved off the path back into the jungle. Ray took over point again—hacking his way through the jungle and eventually I took my turn. I was surprised how tasking it was to hack your way through the undergrowth and the number of thorns, stickers and sharp vines that cut your hands, arms and sometimes your face. And speaking of vines—there were three types. The 'wait a minute vine' would grab you and then let go.

The 'got you vine' would grab you and not let go. And finally a vine we called the 'stomper vine' would grab you, throw you down and when you got back up it would snag you again and throw you down—almost like it was stomping on you.

In the end, that day, we had accomplished our planned movement and had not encountered the enemy. My first day on point was over and I had survived. And I was amazed how much I had learned but how far I had to go to even come close to Ray. He was the master and I was the student. I asked Ray why he didn't seem to be afraid to walk point as he had already been wounded twice. He said 'f ... it—it don't mean nothin' and besides if I get hit again I go back to the rear area—no more combat. There was a rule that if you got three purple hearts they take you out of combat.

Ray was also teaching another guy to walk point, Mike Leeks from the other squad in our platoon. Mike was a surfer from California. As I got to know Mike I found out his Dad was mayor of their town and owned a chain of sporting good stores. Mike talked a lot of his fiancé, Renee as well as surfing and fast cars. Mike was from a 'well to do' family but Mike did not act that way. He seemed more like one of the beach boys with his fast car and surfboard. Mike talked of many times when he and his buddies would cut school and go to the beach and surf. He had owned very nice, fast cars which he loved to polish up for his dates with Renee. He even talked about polishing the windows which made them shine in a very special way. Mike had told his dad he wasn't ready for college and wanted to be a paratrooper. Mike's older brother was a helicopter pilot who served in Vietnam. Mike was a great guy—quick to laugh with a smile on his face. He was like Ray Garza in that way except Mike was not quiet or shy like Ray. Mike was very outgoing and with his good looks he surely had no trouble finding girls. But Mike was true to Renee as they were getting married after Vietnam like Judy and I. And later, after Ray and Smitty were gone, Mike and I became the primary point men for our platoon and we also became best friends.

I walked point two more times with Ray without enemy contact. Ray then told me I was ready to go solo. The next time we had point I would walk it alone. I was excited and scarred as there was a little voice in my head that was saying 'just look at what you've gotten yourself into now, Rick'

Although I was barely beyond being a FNG, I was learning a lot. And probably the most important thing I learned was that everyone in combat is afraid. If you're not you are crazy. The key was to be able to harness your fear into heightened awareness. And when the bullets flew we had to react instantly to overcome the otherwise paralyzing fear.

CHAPTER 3

▼

SOLO AND SO SLOW

Jun 68

Our M/O (method of operation) was basically to be out in the field (combat operations) for 30 to 45 days and then come back to the fire support base for a 5 day stand down (rest) which was not totally rest as we had to guard a portion of the perimeter during this time.

During the time in the field we sometimes might only encounter the enemy a few times when we were in the highlands/jungle. And mostly these encounters were the NVA and often involved firefights—sustained combat with a significant enemy force. When we operated in the low lands (rice paddies and villages) our contact seemed to be more frequent and often was with the VC. These encounters were more guerrilla warfare in the form of snipers and booby traps but sometimes ambushes as well.

Our movement was accomplished by long daily marches, called humps, which were usually 3 to 5 thousand meters or combat assaults with choppers. Either way, at the end of the day we dug our foxholes, filled sand bags and cut trees for our lagger sites—if trees were there. We then constructed our little hooches under which we slept. For our hooches we cut small sticks to which we tied our plastic ponchos making a one-man small tent. These were about 6 feet square and were only about two feet off the ground. It was just high enough for us to slip into with our blown up air mattress (if it didn't have a hole). It would generally keep us dry but did nothing about the malaria laden mosquitoes. We used a light weight camouflaged comforter as a blanket which we pulled over our heads to try to keep the mosquitoes out. These comforters (poncho liners) were specifically designed to dry quickly given the rain and humidity of the jungle.

After digging our perimeter positions we would put out our claymore mines (plastic explosive devices with C-4 as the explosive and a mass of pellets/bb's for shrapnel). We also set trip flares in front of them. Each claymore had a long wire that was connected to a detonating device which we ran back to our foxhole. If the enemy approached us during the night, in theory they would trip the flares and then we would blast them with our claymores.

After building our hooches and eating some c-rations it would get dark. So we would go to sleep after agreeing on a guard schedule. Each of us had to spend two hours guarding our position—mostly during the dead of night. In the jungle it was so dark you couldn't see your hand in front of your face. But you sat by your foxhole with your rifle in one hand and the claymore detonating devise in the other—straining to see or hear anything. Once in a great while we might have someone fall asleep during guard duty. But mostly the fear kept us awake for our two hours. And then in the morning we would pack our stuff up, eat some more c-rations and move out for another march or sometimes a combat assault. If you had a good perimeter, good lagger site, good hooch and an air mattress without a hole, the last thing you wanted to do was leave it all behind and set out again. But we did, over and over and over again.

During my first two or three months of combat operations our enemy contact was mostly in the form of snipers or booby-traps. Once when I was walking point with Ray we were hit by a sniper but it wasn't us who was shot at. To my amazement, the sniper passed up a good shot at me and Ray and waited for our platoon to link up with the point before firing. I guess they wanted a chance to hit more than two of us (me and Ray). But it was chilling to think that Ray and I were in the sights of the snipers weapon and he passed up the shot. But Ray said that happens—especially if there are more than one sniper and/or they feel they will be able to get off multiple good shots before everyone takes cover. Snipers are a form of terrorism as you will be walking along and all of a sudden you will hear the crack of a rifle and see your buddy go down right next to you. Mostly the snipers are well hidden and take off before they can be located, caught or killed.

Booby traps are another form of terrorism because similar to snipers you are walking along and someone hits a booby trap. Mostly they were explosive devices that were triggered by either a pressure plate or a trip wire. The other common booby trap that we encountered was pungi pits. These were holes that were dug in paths or other natural walking spots. In the bottom of the holes they pushed sharpened bamboo stakes into the ground, point up, those were tipped with human feces. These pits were then covered and camouflaged in a manner that made them mostly undetectable. If you fell in a pungi pit usually the stakes would kill you or the infection that set in would disable you and take you out of the field. Both booby traps and snipers mostly involve an invisible enemy that makes it hard to fight back. This is intended to demoralize combat units and allows a few enemy soldiers to affect major disruptions to much larger combat units and their operations.

All Alone on Point
Jun 68

After a couple of months of combat and learning to walk point with Ray, it was my turn to walk point alone. I remember it was in the highlands/jungle. Ray and I got our instructions from the platoon leader and platoon sergeant. Mostly we would be following the path that we had been on but later in the afternoon we would go off into the jungle and on ultimately to the top of a hill for our lagger site. We were told that our intelligence were aware of NVA movement in this area—often along our path. It was just past dawn and I was prepared to take off. Ray was to be second in line.

I remember as I started off I was moving very slowly once I went beyond our perimeter and down the path. I could hear my heart pounding in my chest and I was breathing very heavily. I remember wondering if any American had ever walked down this god-forsaken path in the jungle before me. I had just turned nineteen years old and I was leading a company of 80 or so men into combat. It seemed surreal. I kept looking back at Ray as I slowly walked down the path. Ray would give me the thumbs up sign to encourage me—until I had rounded a corner and could no longer see Ray or anyone else. I was all alone and my senses seemed to be screaming as I strained to see trip wires, pressure devices or enemy soldiers up ahead, or along side the path. Ray told me to stop after 5 minutes for them to link back up to me so I could set out again. After 5 minutes I stopped and waited for them to link up with me. But my wait was not long as I had gone very, very slowly. When Ray linked up he told me I would have to go faster. I said OK but I knew the faster I went, the further I went all alone and the more likely I was to not see something (trip wires, enemy, etc). But I did speed up a little. But when Ray linked up again he said I was still too slow and that I needed to speed up and I did.

And as far as being all alone point, it was a very scary place for me because I had developed a deathly fear of being captured. A lot of guys had an M-16 round in their helmet band. I asked what it was for. They told me it was in case you ran out of ammo and were going to get captured—better off dead. I put a round in my helmet band—and I was very serious. No way was I going to be captured.

As the day wore on and I continued on point until late in the afternoon I was told to get off the path and use a map and compass to navigate through the jungle. So I took off again with a machete in one hand and my M16 in the other. I hacked my way through a mass of vines, small trees, stickers and underbrush, all of which tore at my hands, arms and face. It was very slow going and extremely tiresome. At one point as I hacked my way through a tangle of vines and dense underbrush I tripped and fell forward into a gigantic spider web. It engulfed me. I hollered for Ray and he came and helped me out of that mess. As I was shaking off the webs a giant spider came down from some of the remaining webs. Its body was bigger than my fist. The jungles of Vietnam were a living hell hole—one nightmare after another.

All 80 men behind you on point followed the path that you had hacked out through the jungle. Again, I was told to speed up. Ray told me to only clear enough to get through and he would widen the path behind me for the rest of the company. That worked and we finally made it to our planned lagger site. I was so tired I thought I might die. It was not only the physical exertion of hacking through the jungle but also the fear and stress of not knowing what lied ahead the entire day. My first solo on point was uneventful from an enemy contact standpoint—but it was solo, so slow and so tiring. But I had done it—and Ray was proud of me.

CHAPTER 4

▼

BASE CAMP/SIN CITY/USO SHOWS

Base Camp

When we were back in base camp during a stand-down, we had guard duty along the perimeter but this was only for 2 or 3 hours a day. So mostly we rested and took in easy. It didn't take long to realize that back in base camp most of the guys either drank beer or smoked pot. I was only 18 so I had had a few cans of beer before but nothing much. And the beer was almost always warm. When it was 90+ degrees and humid, warm beer tasted horrible to many of us. So Ray introduced me to pot. We were in the perimeter bunker and he gave me a marijuana cigarette. I smoked it and felt nothing and I told Ray 'this was nothing'. He told me to inhale deeply and hold it in my lungs for 10 second or so. After doing this twice the next thing I knew I was laughing uncontrollably. Ray and the other guys were laughing too—probably at me. So that was my introduction to pot. Most of us who smoked pot in Vietnam had never done so before and probably never did so after. Although illegal, mostly the officers looked the other way as long as there was no trouble. For the most part guys would smoke pot for a bit, get goofy and then get hungry (we called it the munchies or the rabbit.), eat and then go to sleep. You could get pot right outside the base camp from the kids who were selling coke (Coca Cola), beer, etc on the black market. It was very cheap with a pack (20) of marijuana cigarettes costing $5.00 and it was easier to get than cold beer. I never saw any fights when guys were smoking marijuana. Whereas, the guys drinking beer would get drunk, mean and have great big fights. It seemed ironic that the legal warm beer ultimately caused fights and a lot of trouble. Whereas the illegal pot caused guys to mellow out, have some laughs and never created any trouble. However, there were a few guys who apparently had used drugs back in the states and took the opportunity in Vietnam to do a lot of drugs including opium, heroin and LSD. But when we were out in the field there was little to no drinking or drug use.

One guy, Sky Skyler, had a tendency to get into trouble no matter where he was or what he was doing. One time in base camp Sky had smoked so much pot he got the rabbit big time. Unfortunately we were going back in the field within the next couple of days and they had distributed our C-rations early. Well, Sky commenced to sit down and eat a week's worth of C-rations all at one time. The next morning he was asking who had eaten his C-rations and we told him he had and he said he did feel kind of full. So Sky had to beg us for some of ours. That wasn't a problem because we tended to throw away about half of our meals—keeping only the best stuff and tossing the rest as it was too heavy and not wanted. And you guessed right, Sky ended up with the rejected stuff but he didn't seem to much care. This was the same guy who spent 5 nights in jail on his

R&R to Hong Kong as he raped a whore for whom he claimed he had paid but who then she decided not to put out. Somehow, someway trouble always seemed to find Sky. Some might say Sky had bad luck. Others might say bad luck follows those who make bad choices. Either way, Sky had more than his share of trouble and bad luck.

Ty Taylor and JJ

Sin City

Just outside our base camp at Ahn Khe was a group of bars/hang-outs that was affectionately known as Sin City. Why this place was not 'off-limits' was beyond me. Not only could you get cold beer and liquor but drugs and prostitution was rampant and very much out in the open. We would go into these bars and pretty soon young Vietnamese whores would come up to the GI's, get in their laps offering them pot and a variety of sexual favors, of course for a price. To say Sin City was aptly named was a gross understatement. During the 5 days or so we were on our stand-downs in Ahn Khe we would generally make one trip to Sin City and just check things out for a laugh. Some guys would get involved with the whores but it was a risky proposition as you were as likely as not to end up with some type of V.D—mostly clap. So Ray and some of us would go to Sin City and just walk around, going into bars and watching as GI's would make fools of themselves getting involved with the whores and probably ending up with more than they bargained for. Ultimately the Army made Sin City off-limits probably because they were running low on penicillin. What was really scary is they told us there were certain strains of V.D. that you could get in Vietnam that were incurable and would preclude you from going home. Rumor had it that GI's with those types of V.D. were sent to some remote island where they were quarantined indefinitely. It almost sounded like a leper colony. We didn't know how true this was but it was enough for most of us to stay away from the whores, especially those who had girl friends or wives at home.

USO Shows

Nearly all of the GI's who were sent to Vietnam thought they would get to see Bob Hope and his USO show. It didn't take us long to realize that Bob Hope only went to the biggest/safest base camps so most of us never saw him. It was fairly common for other USO shows to be held at some of the smaller base camps such as Ahn Khe. During the time Ahn Khe was our base camp there was one USO show that we had the opportunity to see during one of our stand downs. Ray and I went to it and we were amazed how good it was to see American women who we referred to as 'round eyes'. The performers sang a couple of songs and then the lead singer, a beautiful blonde sang 'To Sir with Love' and brought the house down. I'll never forget it and it made me sad when it was over as we were so very, very far from home and the beautiful girl friends we had left behind.

CHAPTER 5

▼

OPERATION COCHISE— DISASTER

In August, about 4 months into my combat experience we had just ended one of our stand-downs when we conducted another combat assault into the lowlands not too far from Bon Song (a small Vietnamese city close to LZ (landing zone) Uplift). This area was known to be a VC stronghold and the name of our operation was operation Cochise. Why it was called that I do not know. But the mission was another search and destroy mission—search out the Viet Cong and destroy them. That was easier said than done, however. There were many small villages amongst the rice paddies but every village had no young men— only women, children and an occasional 'papa son' (grandpa). Of course there was a reason for no men, they were VC and were either hiding out or were out on missions which were basically killing and maiming our buddies.

Ray's Death
Aug 68

One afternoon after setting up our perimeter for the night, we were re-supplied by helicopters (Hueys) and the battalion commander was dropped off to spend a few days with some of his troops during Operation Cochise. The next morning Ray Garza was going to walk point again, one last time with 16 days left in Vietnam. I remember Ray waking up that morning and he told me he was so short that he couldn't see over his c-ration can. He had some RVN 'Kit Carson' scouts with him on point. We also had a German Shepard with us and a dog handler who were next in line after Ray. Ray set out on point with the dog and dog handler right behind. The rest of his squad followed and my squad was next in line being part of Mike platoon. Ray was moving slowly that morning as there were bobby traps reportedly in this area. Late in the morning Ray was told that the battalion commander wanted him to speed up—we were going too slowly. Ray increased his pace somewhat but was told again to go even faster. But the dog kept alerting on the scent of the 'Kit Carsons' which were false alerts. So when the dog alerted to the booby trap Ray assumed it was another false alert. All of a sudden there was a terrific explosion; you could feel the ground shake. Then there was silence which was immediately followed by screaming. Then others started yelling 'booby traps'. We were told to freeze and stay where we were. But I knew Ray was on point and I had to go up to see about him. Smitty told me not to go to Ray because I shouldn't see him like that. But I did. Ray had stepped on a booby trapped 105 artillery round which blew a hole through him the size of a football. Ray was still somewhat alive but clearly was not going to live. I laid down next to Ray waiting for the medic who I knew couldn't help. One guy named Rosey had his arm almost blown off. Several others were dead or severely wounded. The dog handler and his dog were right behind Ray. Smitty turned the dog handler over so the Doc could patch him up. That's when his internal organs just sloughed out and he said 'God it hurts'. Doc hit him with morphine and he just drifted out and died. His dog was next to him and already dead. As it turned out the dog handler had two days left in Vietnam and his wife was waiting for him in Hawaii. I stayed with Ray until the helicopters came. I helped put Ray in the helicopter and some of the others. We placed the dog handler in a poncho and then wondered what to do with the dog. Someone said to put the dog with him so we laid the dog on top of the dog handler in the same poncho. This was the saddest day of my life. Not only losing a best friend but there was something about the dog and dog handler that haunts me to this day. It seemed like dogs weren't supposed to die in Vietnam—as if people were. The helicopters took off and they told us to saddle up. Smitty took point and we started moving again—as if nothing had happened. I cried. Ray was right; he left combat and went home with his 3d Purple Heart—in a body bag. Now I knew first hand how deadly serious it was to walk point. Point had taken my best friend when he only had 16 days left in that God forsaken hell-hole, Vietnam. Point had also taken a dog and his handler. None of this seemed fair and should not have happened—not even in a war. But I learned right then and there was nothing fair about 'point'. 'Point was deadly and badder than bad'.

Ray Garza—3 Purple Hearts

Smitty Ambushed/Mike Platoon Wiped Out
Aug 68

The next couple of days were uneventful. Then we set up our perimeter in a cemetery just outside a village which of course had no men. Obviously they were V.C. At the end of the third day following Ray's death we were digging our foxholes when the platoon leader came by and wanted to talk with us about sending out an ambush that night. One of our squad leaders, Glenn said he was too sick with malaria to take out an ambush so the lieutenant wants volunteers. Smitty and I were fire team leaders and he asked us whose turn it was and who wanted to do the ambush. We both hesitated, I kind of thought it might have been our turn but finally Smitty said 'f ...—it—we'll do it. Don't mean nothin'. Smitty, as I mentioned was a seasoned combat veteran having survived some huge battles including Dak To. Also, as one of our primary point men, he knew his stuff very well. (I thought Ray might have taught Smitty to walk point because Smitty was very good. But Smitty said the guys who taught him to walk point were all dead.) In the early afternoon Smitty and Dickson went to check out the ambush site when a kid shows up with a huge infected eye. He kept saying 'Bac Shee' which means can't see. They took him to our perimeter to find Doc and the CO jumped their asses for bringing him in without a blindfold. Smitty figured he was blind but as it turned out he saw plenty. The ambush site was good but it was too out in the open. The villagers apparently saw them as they went out to the site as there was no other way to get there. So Smitty took Glenn's men and Jimmy Dickson out to the ambush site after dark that night and just as they were approaching their ambush site they were ambushed. Jimmy had the radio as he was to have 1st watch. The satchel charge that killed Jimmy also took out the radio so there was no communication but we knew something had happened as we heard this explosion and a bunch of automatic weapons fire. We heard a few more explosions and then there was nothing. At about this same time our perimeter was mortared with numerous shells hitting within the command post area. The commanding officer's RTO was hit. And then there was nothing for a very long time and finally the orders came down for us to go out to the ambush site to get our guys as they should have been back by now after the enemy contact. Someone said they heard that Smitty had called on the radio saying 'come out and get us—everyone is dead, everyone's dead'. So we took a fire-team out and we set out after Smitty and his guys. The enemy was gone but our guys were a mess. When we found Smitty he was wounded but he said to take care of Jimmy who was dying. In total five of the six guys were hit. Jimmy died, one guy was blinded, two others had fairly serious wounds and Smitty was saying he had a million dollar wound in his leg and was going home. And as for Smitty's call on the radio—it never happened as the radio was dead. Where this had come from is not known. But there is a lot of confusion and chaos when guys got hit— especially at night.

We carried them back to the perimeter and called in helicopters for a medivac. This medivac was dead in the middle of the night. We popped flares and the chopper came in with its search lights blazing. All of this was surely giving away our position to the enemy which normally we would never do. However, when you have guys hurt as bad as this, you do whatever you can to get them out and to the hospital. And it was pretty obvious the enemy knew where we were as they had just mortared our position.

Smitty was still saying he was OK but it was so dark—we couldn't see anything. Little did we know that his leg wound had hit an artery and he had big time shrapnel in his back. He almost bled out and went into a coma in the chopper on the way back to the base camp. I later learned that Smitty had spent 6 months in the hospital in the states as the result of his 'million dollar wound'.

Smitty

So then, of the 20 or so guys we started out with in Mike platoon, there were only 7 of us left—our platoon had effectively been wiped-out and we were disbanded to other platoons. And the irony was that Smitty was finally headed for his R&R in Australia and Dickson to his 'in country R&R' at Vung Tau—both the next day. And of course the next morning we were told pack it up we're moving out—as if nothing had happened. But something had happened—our platoon had been wiped out and guess where it had come from—the V.C. village.

The next day as we set up our perimeter the 7 of us from Mike platoon started talking. As it turned out this was the second time Mike platoon had been wiped out. The first time (before me) was in Feb '68 at BanMe Thout. Mike platoon was sent to recon a NVA Regimental command post. They ended up surrounded, cut off and decimated. The only thing that had saved the four who walked out of there was two Huey guns ship that hovered right on top of the four and opened up with their mini-guns. Two of the four guys who walked out of there were Ray and Smitty and now they were gone. The more we talked the more convinced we were that not only the men from that village (who were nowhere to be found) were at fault but the whole village. We were pretty sure one of the kids had tipped off the ambush site and who knew who could have set the booby trap. The talk became very serious about going back through that village and killing everyone and everything in sight. We had never done anything like that before, but we had never seen all of our buddies killed and maimed like this. Someone had to pay and they were the right ones—no question. As this talk started to develop into a serious plan, our lieutenant came over to us and said he wanted to talk to us. He said he had heard what we were considering and even though in many ways he felt it might be justified—in the end it would not end up being justified. No matter the reason, killing all the women and children in a village would be a war crime and we would all be court martialled and go to jail. Someone said 'so what, sometimes you have to do what you have to do'. But others of us started realizing that no matter how much we felt this was justified, others would not. And later, we realized the lieutenant was right. Thank God for this lieutenant, he kept us from doing a horrible thing and ruining our lives. But to this day, I still believe in my mind that it would have been justified—at the time. And in some ways I almost feel guilty that we had let our buddies down by not avenging their deaths. Yet, I am glad we did not do it. This whole thing was insane. We were only 19 and 20 year old kids—making life and death decisions in a war that we were not being allowed to win. (We wanted to get orders to proceed north to Hanoi, invading North Vietnam. With the support of our superior fire power (Air Force, Navy and our Army helicopters), and all of the U.S. army and marine infantry forces, we felt we could have crushed the NVA, took Hanoi and ended the war in 6 months. With no NVA support, the Viet Cong would have disbanded and become a non-factor)

The Mai Lai massacre happened a couple of years after my return from Vietnam. In Mai Lai, after seeing their buddies killed and maimed by a village, they did go through the village and killed everyone including women and children. The difference in our situation, than in Mai Lai, was our lieutenant talked us out of it. In Mai Lai, their lieutenant joined them in the killing. I totally understand how this happened. But our lieutenant was right, no matter how justified it seemed at the time, it would have been viewed as a war crime.

*Rick Butler & Pete Milner—survivors from
Mike platoon—taken after Ray Garza's
memorial service*

CHAPTER 6

▼

CAUTIOUS BUT
GETTING GOOD
& FASTER

After operation Cochise we went up into the highlands and jungle again. There were numerous intelligence reports of significant NVA activity in this one area. Again we encountered triple canopy jungles covering hill after hill. Our squad was on point again when we came upon a very rocky hill that was covered with huge boulders. We found some paths that led into the boulders so we followed them. We found the paths lead to tunnels that went down under many of the boulders. I was not the point man that day but we were the point squad so we ended up going into the tunnels behind the point man. These were very small tunnels which required us to crawl on our hands a knees. They were also very dark. We couldn't see anything and only knew we were going the right way because occasionally we'd bump into the guy in front of us. Of all the things we had to do during combat operations in Vietnam, going into these tunnels was one of the hardest things we did. Everything inside you says don't do this—something very bad could happen down in those pitch black tunnels. It was terrifying to say the least. But we did it and the one with the most guts that day was our point man as usual.

NVA Hospital
Sep 68

At various points along the tunnels we encountered large openings—like underground rooms. We found used medical supplies which made us believe we were onto some kind of a medical clinic or hospital and likely NVA or Viet Cong. Finally our point man encountered the enemy. There was small arms fire (M16 and AK47's and some explosions (which turned out to be grenades). All of this was deafening within the tunnel complex. Then the word came to back up and get out. But the tunnels were so tight we could not turn around and had to back out until we encountered one of the rooms. It was there the point man told us that he had come upon a very big room that was lit and had guards. It was an NVA hospital. As soon as our point man came out of the tunnel the guards spotted him and they exchanged fire. Our guy then threw a couple of hand grenades and came back. He thought this was a very big NVA hospital. So we came back out of the tunnels and radioed the platoon leader and informed him of our findings. He talked with the commanding officer and we were ordered to get out of the rocks as we were going to call in artillery. As it turned out the USS New Jersey, a Navy battleship, was just off the coast very near us. So they fired their 16 inch guns and we zeroed them in on the tunnel and rock complex that housed the NVA hospital. The artillery was coming straight over our heads and the 16 inch shells sounded like freight trains as they passed over us. Some hit close enough that you could feel the concussion and the ground would shake—sometimes lifting us up off the ground. It was getting dark so we set up our perimeter, dug our foxholes, laggered in and waited. They decided to continue the shelling throughout the night to keep the NVA from escaping out of the tunnels.

JJ's Short Round
Sep 68

One of the guys in our squad was named John Jacobs (JJ). JJ was from Virginia and was a very nice toe headed guy with a baby face and a southern drawl. He looked like he belonged in high school not in a war. One time while waiting in line for chow at base camp JJ had nearly been killed by a short round. (A short round is an artillery round that does not go as far as the other rounds and falls short—often on friendly troops.) Guys before and after JJ were hurt but remarkably he was untouched. One guy was killed by this short round and another FNG was hit by shrapnel that drove his dog tags into his stomach. The shrapnel was all around JJ and he was knocked down by the blast from the short round but was unhurt. This was the beginning of an obsession that JJ had about short rounds. And JJ would tell anybody who would listen that there was a short round out there somewhere with his name on it that was going to get him. Well the night of the NVA hospital shelling JJ was on his watch, guarding our perimeter, when his short round came. Had JJ been inside the foxhole which was covered with logs and sand bags, he would have been fine (and some might have said that it wasn't his short round). But JJ, like a lot of us at that point, was not a FNG. So he was sitting on top of the sand bags with his steel pot (helmet) on and his M16. Well, as it turned out, this was JJ's short round. The round (from one of the New Jersey's 16 inch guns) hit right in front of our foxhole. We all heard and felt the tremendous explosion and I knew JJ was on guard duty and that this was his short round. We scrambled to our foxhole and found JJ in the bottom of it. He wasn't moving and we lit a match and saw him laying in the bottom of the foxhole, all black from the blast. Then it seemed a dead man or a ghost started moving and miraculously it got up. But somehow it wasn't a ghost or a dead man. It was JJ and he had managed to survive his short round. Once JJ realized he was alive, a great big smile came on his blackened face and he said 'that was my short round and it missed me'. Someone said to JJ that it must not have truly been his short round or it would have gotten him. JJ would hear none of that and he kept saying 'that was my short round and it missed me. I'm going to be OK now.' And you know he really believed this. JJ had about 20 days or so to go in Vietnam when this happened. Our CO (commanding officer) heard this and told JJ to get on the next chopper and go back to the base camp for the rest of his time. But JJ would have no part of it. He even wanted to walk point because he kept saying and believing he had dodged the grim reaper and he would be fine. I remember him coming up to me and saying in his 'JJ type of way' (he spoke slowly and all drawled out in his Virginian accent)—"Sergeant Fredrick Lee Butler, that was my short round. And it wasn't a small mortar round. No-no, it was a 16 inch monster shell from the battleship USS New Jersey. It sounded like a freight train and had 'JJ' written all over it. And the grim reaper was riding that bastard as it came in on me. I saw him with his black hooded cloak, his cycle and his big teeth.

But can you believe it? Somehow I managed to dodge that son-of—a-bitch and I actually saw the smile go off his ugly face. And he's not coming back for me because there are no more short rounds with JJ written on them. I'm gonna be fine now and go home." And he was. JJ went home back to Virginia 20 days later. He had a piece of shrapnel in his pocket that he now called his good luck charm. JJ had dug this out of one of the logs he had been sitting on when he was blown back into the foxhole. I'd like to say that JJ's good luck charm gave him good luck for the rest of his life. But I have no way of knowing as I never saw JJ again. But I would be willing to bet that JJ still has that piece of shrapnel. And to anyone who will listen, he shows it as he forever tells his story of how he dodged that grim reaper son-of-a-bitch and the short round with JJ written all over it.

JJ dodged the Grim Reaper

The next morning after JJ's infamous short round, we went back to the tunnels and rocks. Although many of the tunnels were caved in due to the artillery, many were still in tact given the fortification of those huge boulders. We went inside and found many of the NVA were dead and others were in very bad shape having been concussed severely by the artillery fire. This was in fact a huge NVA hospital and one of the most interesting things we found was $1million in greenbacks (our squad found the money). We were not sure what this money was for but we turned it in. We thought of keeping at least some of it but the currency used by GI's in Vietnam was known as MPC (military payment certificates) and we were forbidden to have green-backs. You might have thought we would have received some kind of medal for all of this. Instead our squad was chosen as the squad of the month and we had steak dinner and ice cream with the commanding general of the 173d. And I think, to the man, each of us would have chosen the steak and ice cream over any medal at that point. As far as getting to meet the general, I think we could have pretty much cared less—don't mean noth-ing. And only recently I heard that some guys from the 50th Mechanized Infantry had applied for rights to the $150,000 they found in a hospital cave in a Suoi Ca operation and were successful in recovering the money. I guess we never thought to try to recover any of the $1 million we found. Or, if anyone did, they left me out and I don't know anything about it. Either way, I think the statute of limitations has probably run out by now. What is the saying 'the spoils of war go to the victors'. Well, we sure didn't feel like victors and I doubt the United States did either at the end of this war.

We continued our search and destroy operations over the next few months. Much of this was in the highlands and some in the lowlands. Mike and I walked point many times during this period and we were getting better, faster and more confident. Also, we conducted many C.A.'s . I don't know how many C.A.'s I did in Vietnam but it must have been a big number. Because it took 27 CA's to get an air medal. And we got ours after being in combat only about 3 to 4 months.

CHAPTER 7

▼

VERY GOOD, FAST AND BECOMING DANGEROUS

It was September and I had been in Vietnam for 6 months. I had walked point numerous times and was very good, confident and fast. Becoming fast on point was not necessarily a good thing. In fact the faster you are the more dangerous it becomes. We were now back in the lowlands not too far from Bong Song. The terrain was flat—mostly rice paddies punctuated periodically by villages which were no more than a group of grass huts.

POW's
Sep 68

I was on point again and I was moving quickly but very quietly as I approached a village. Everything was dead quiet & I wondered if it was deserted. The first grass hut I came to I entered and couldn't believe my eyes when I saw 7 young Vietnamese men sitting around a kettle eating rice. I immediately assumed they were V.C. & told them to put their hands up. One of them started to move so I shot a burst from my M16 (on fully automatic) through the roof of the hut & yelled for my squad to help me. I had just single-handedly captured 7 POW.s. We brought in South Vietnamese interrogators. At first they did not want to talk. However, the interrogators took three of them up in a helicopter and asked them questions again. The first two POW's still wouldn't talk and they were pushed out of the helicopter. The third one decided he had better talk so he did. And what he said was consistent with documents we had taken off one of them. So, they were, in fact, V.C. with one being a high ranking officer. It was very unusual to capture POW's in this war—let alone 7.

I had heard that you got an in-country R&R at Vung Tao for capturing a POW. I was then told I would get 7 R&R's for my efforts. I could hardly believe it as it seemed too good to be true. As it turned out it was too good to be true. They came back and told me the two they had pushed out of the helicopter no longer counted. (I suspect the official records showed we had only captured 5 POW's) So now they said I would get 5 R&R's. I thought that still sounded very good. And then they came back and told me I wouldn't get any R&R's because they had to have their weapons with them when I captured them. Their weapons were buried in straw and pig shit outside their houch (straw hut). Later somebody asked me if I got at least a Silver Star for capturing 7 POW's. My answer was no medals, no R&R's, no nothing—the Army—go figure. But I really think there would have been a medal for me but someone got nervous about how many POW's to put on the citation.

Parachute Jumps/Jump Master School
Sep 68

It wasn't long after the POW incident that word came down that they were starting up a jump master school at Camp Radcliff (Ahn Khe). The reason for starting the jump master school was the 173d was the only unit drawing jump pay so they had to be prepared to jump. In order to jump we had to have a certain number of jump masters which we did not have. Out of our battalion (about 500 men) they selected 4 of us to go including me. I told the asst battalion commander to send someone else because I was getting burned out and was going to terminate my jump status after Vietnam. He said no, they wanted me to go so I did. They didn't say this was my reward for the POW's but having thought about it, I think somehow it was. In any event, I attended the 1 week school and made three parachute jumps—all training jumps out of Huey helicopters. The only other jumps any of us had made were out of C119 propeller planes in jump school. You would think the Army would have told us that it would be way different jumping out of a helicopter because you do not have nearly the horizontal air speed or prop blast that causes your chute to nearly explode as it opens violently out of the C119. We were always told to count to 5 after exiting the plane (one thousand one, one thousand two …) and if your chute is not open at 5 to pull the handle on our emergency reserve chute. Out of a C119 your chute exploded open before you could say three. But out of the Hueys, I counted to 5 and was starting to pull my reserve chute as I felt just a little tug and I looked up and saw my chute slowly starting to open. If I would have counted a split second faster I would have pulled my reserve chute and it would have likely tangled in my other chute and often neither open and you die. The Army—go figure. On my last jump I was headed toward a river in the middle of the drop zone as I was coming down. They tell you if you're going to land in water to use your quick release on your harness to drop out of it at about 10–15' so your chute will not come down on your head and drown you. Well the river wasn't very wide and it was only at the last minute I realized I was going into the water. So my chute came down on my head & I started struggling—afraid I was drowning when all of a sudden my foot hit the bottom. The water level was up to my neck so I walked out of the river.

Ambush/No Bronze Stars
Sep 68

Back in early August, 1968 (before operation Cochise) they held a review board for promotions to Sgt E5 (buck sergeant). We were short on NCOs (non-commissioned officers) because of our many recent casualties. During the review board they asked each of us separately the same questions concerning combat situations. One of the questions they asked us is what would we do if your squad comes under intense fire from an ambush. The answer is you immediately establish fire superiority by shooting back on full automatic. Once you have obtained fire superiority over the enemy you can move out of the kill zone, call in artillery on the enemy position, etc. This is not the normal reaction to being ambushed. You have a tendency to either run or to take cover and wait. Either of these options are not good because you are likely still in the kill zone and the enemy fire will soon take you out. This question and its answer proved very pertinent to us about a month later when our squad walked into an ambush. Mike Leeks and I were by each other in the point squad. We were walking along a dike in a rice paddy when the ambush came from a nearby tree line. Two of our guys were hit immediately and we went down behind the low dike for cover. Mike and I knew we were in the kill zone so we immediately returned fire on full automatic while the others continued to stay down behind what little cover we had. After a couple of minutes we had gained fire superiority and the enemy stopped shooting. At this point Mike was on his last magazine and I had three left after we each started out with 11 magazines with 18 rounds in each. Towards the end I had switched to single shot from full automatic because I was afraid I was going to run out of ammo. My M16 also jammed slightly when we initially dove for cover but I got it cleared. So in 2 or three minutes Mike and I had returned fire totaling over 300 rounds. Apparently the enemy became discouraged and took off. They put Mike and me in for Bronze Stars for our actions but we never heard anything more about any medals. The Army—go figure.

Mike Leeks & Rick Butler

Listening Post (LP)/Tanks
Sep 68

It wasn't long after the ambush that we hooked up with a tank company (M60 tanks). This was a welcome break for us because instead of walking with our heavy packs we got to ride on the tanks. We initially were right along the coast of the South China Sea. We actually set up a perimeter once right on the beach and went swimming. And I remember thinking although it was a beautiful sandy beach, there were no life guards and it sure wasn't a public beach. It was a remote beach in an isolated part of Vietnam. I remember wondering what might be in the water. But ultimately the little voice that I had started hearing in my head said 'f ... it—don't mean nothin'. So I went in the water and went swimming. We moved inland into some small hills but not into the deep jungle. We had made contact with some NVA elements and had engaged them in some fire fights but the contact mostly was light. One night we set up our perimeter with the tanks on the top of a hill. Our squad was ordered to put out an LP (listening post). This is where 3 or 4 guys go out in front of the perimeter after dark possibly 50 to 75 yards and set up for the night. The LP has a radio and its mission is to listen for enemy advancement toward the perimeter and to give warning of the same. This was a very dangerous assignment as you did not have enough fire power to engage the enemy and your only option once contact was made would be to run back to your perimeter before you were shot or captured. I took two of the guys from my squad with me and left our perimeter. We set up the listening post and once again it was so dark you couldn't see your hand in front of your face. We decided on the order in which we would pull guard duty. I was first on guard duty which meant I had to stay awake and then wake up the second guy who in turn would wake up the last guy. At the end of my 2 hour shift I woke up James, made sure he was awake and gave him the radio. I then went to sleep. The next thing I knew James was waking me up and whispered 'we've got movement'. I said where and he pointed towards the perimeter. He had fallen asleep and the enemy had gotten by us and was between us and our tanks. Talk about being terrified, the fear was nearly overwhelming. My heart was beating so hard I thought the enemy would hear it. This was my worst nightmare coming true—I thought for sure we were going to be captured. My fear had nearly taken my breath away but I got on the radio and told the tank commander our predicament. He asked if there was anything we could get in front of because he wanted to shoot a canister round (like a huge shot gun shell) right at us. This way they would get the enemy and clear a path for us to return to our perimeter. I said we were right behind a huge boulder and he told us to get in front of it and when we were ready to radio them. We did so and when I radioed back he said for us to be sure to yell friendlies as we were running back to the perimeter otherwise we would be shot. They fired the tank's canister round right at us. The sound and concussion was deafening but we immediately got up and ran straight up the hill toward the tanks yelling friendly, friendly as we approached. We made it back without getting shot or captured. The next morning we searched the area in front of our position and found numerous blood trails indicating that we had killed or wounded some of the enemy but they had carried them off as they often would do. The blood trails were between our LP sight and the tanks. No-one had to tell me how lucky we were to have made it back and not to have been captured. JJ was deathly afraid of short-rounds and I was deathly afraid of being captured.

We stayed at this perimeter for a few more nights and were running patrols during the day. The day after our listening post incident (above) we started getting intelligence that indicated there were regimental size NVA forces very near our position. Even though we had tanks with our company we became concerned that such a significant force could get close enough to us at night to easily over-run our position. Although listening posts and trip flares were designed to give us notice of the advancing enemy, the concern was that it would not be enough advance warning. Consequently the next few nights were as bright as day due to our artillery shooting large flares on parachutes that constantly kept the whole area fully illuminated. It was kind of eerie as the flares would dangle back and forth beneath their parachutes causing shadows to dance across the area. It seemed surreal and very scary as we never before were concerned about being over-run—especially not with tanks. But apparently the tanks were a deterrent as we encountered small numbers of NVA a couple of times during patrols but no significant force.

No Food or Water/Banished from Base Camp
Oct 68

We stayed with the tanks for about a month which ended when we made a C.A. up into the highlands again. Our landing zone was a clearing on top of a hill that had deep elephant grass. Before we went in the door gunner told us it was a hot L.Z. (landing zone) as the gun ships that had strafed the L.Z. had return fire. As we went in there was small arms fire and the door gunner right next to me was shot in the shoulder. We hovered about 5 feet above the elephant grass and we jumped off. Then we found out that the elephant grass was about 7 feet high so we plunged 10 to 12 feet through the elephant grass to the ground. There was shooting but mostly chaos as you couldn't see anything but the elephant grass which was over our heads. Finally we got organized into a perimeter as the other choppers came down. One of the choppers was shot down after they dropped our guys off. No-one in that chopper survived as it went up in a ball of fire.

We then commenced to move through the jungle for the next week and a half. The jungle terrain here was unlike anything we had seen before. There were steep hills that sometimes almost formed canyons and yet the top of these canyons were covered by the jungle canopies. As we approached one such canyon a huge tree had fallen across the top—bridging this small canyon that was probably 100 feet deep. The point man (from a different platoon) decided to cross by walking on the fallen tree. The tree was about 3 feet wide and was covered with moss. It didn't seem like it was slippery although it looked like it was. We crossed one man at a time to minimize the weight on the tree because it was creaking as each man crossed. This was very scary and treacherous as evidenced by one of our guys falling to his death in that canyon. They sent one medic with a radio down to check him but he was dead. We then had to call in a helicopter with a jungle penetrator which we used to extract his body from the canyon and jungle. I remember we popped smoke (colored smoke grenades) to signal where the chopper should lower the penetrator. It took about 4 times to finally get the penetrator in the right position and extract the body.

As a point man I wouldn't have chosen to cross the canyon on that tree. I believed that point men needed to be concerned about the security and safety of all 80 men in our company. But some guys who walked point thought they were hot shots and liked to show off their stuff. Or, maybe the C.O. or a platoon leader ordered him to cross on the tree. But even so, if he hadn't wanted to, I doubt they would have made him. I didn't ask and was not told.

After the extraction we continued and came across one of the last creeks we would encounter for quite a while. The water was cool, clear and refreshing. So we drank our fill and filled our canteens only to then find a dead, bloated enemy body around the bend in the creek—upstream. Many guys got violently sick. We weren't sure whether it was the water or the idea of the body. I suspect it was the idea of the body because we all had drunk and less than half of us got sick. Just one more thing to add to the list of Vietnam horrors.

We continued through deep jungle and had not been re-supplied for quite a while as we were unable to find any type of clearing. We also had not crossed any rivers so we ran out of food and water. I remember not having any water for at least two days and no food for about 3 days. We had been licking the dew drops off of leaves in the morning—anything to get some water and when we finally came to a clearing and a small village I saw guys drink water right out of the rice paddies. Not only was the water rancid but the rice paddies are fertilized with human excrement. That's how desperate we were. At one point I had a 'wet one' (an alcohol swab) and I opened it and sucked on it for the moisture. Finally the choppers came in with food and water and our other re-supplies. The 'hot chow' they brought us from the base camp was cold and had grease floating on it. The guys got really pissed at the cooks in the base camp. We thought anyone in the base camp was 'getting over' (getting off easy) and the guys said they were going to make those cooks pay for getting over and sending out the crap chow to us.

Well it was a full 45 days since we had left base-camp before we returned. But the guys had not forgot about the cooks getting over. And when we got back to base-camp we lined up for hot chow at the mess hall. But it was just after dinner and the cooks refused to feed us. Anyway, that first night back in base camp (Camp Radcliff in Ahn Khe) a bunch of our guys got drunk and at 2:00 AM all hell broke loose—all kinds of small arms and machine gun fire and explosions. Everyone thought the base camp had been over-run by the enemy. But that had not happened. Some of our guys decided to ambush the mess hall to get the cooks. They almost blew the mess hall down and thankfully there was only one cook in there and he was only slightly wounded. I'm not sure who all had done this—definitely guys from our company and mostly from our platoon. The guys who had perpetrated the mess hall ambush dunked their weapons in a vat of JP-4 cleaning fluid that was by the barracks just before the MP's caught up with them at the barracks. They called a formation at 4:00 AM and checked all of our rifles to see whose had been fired (all had been cleaned when we came in the previous day). All of the weapons looked to have been cleaned but the MP's were all over us and knew we had done this. As a result the battalion commander decided to relieve our commanding officer of his command. Another factor in our commanding officer being relieved was the time he had refused an order for us to move further in the jungle when we were out of food and water. Our company was banished from the base camp and we had to set up a perimeter just outside for the rest of our stand-down and for future stand-downs. We were never allowed back in the base camp. But that morning as we were packing up our stuff some of the guys went over to the cooks in what was left of the mess hall and told them 'any more cold greasy food and we're coming back'. And you know what; the cooks knew we meant it.

I wasn't a part of the ambush on the mess hall. But I understood how and why it happened. You train guys to be killers. You put them in horrendous conditions with little food or water. They are fighting a mostly invisible enemy who hits and runs. They watch their buddies getting blown up and killed. And it all combines to make you half crazy and turns you into an animal. And then they wonder why things like this happen.

We never did get back into Camp Radcliff. Our banishment was for real so we made our perimeter outside the base-camp until we finally were reassigned to LZ Uplift. It was a fire-support base—not really a base-camp but it was the best we got after the mess hall ambush. I also found out that this was not the first time we had been banished from a base-camp. Back in January of '68 our company was banished from Camp Enari in Pleiku for burning down a Fourth Infantry EM (enlisted men) club. This was before my time and I don't know the details. But I do know that the mess hall made it our second banishment. I never heard of a company being banished from its base camp before. And it happened to us twice Maybe we were the worst of the worst. But being mean and ruthless was not all that bad a quality for a combat unit. So in other ways maybe we were the best of the best....

River Crossing
Oct 68

On one of our next missions we were back in the lowlands. It was very different terrain than the rice paddies we were used to.

It almost looked like a prairie and at one point there were 2 or 3 large rivers that converged. I was walking point again and wouldn't you know we needed to cross the river. No-one knew how deep it was so they tied a rope around my waist and told me to cross and if I went in over my head, they would pull me out. I took off all my gear except my helmet and crossed with my rifle above my head—kind of like I've seen in some war movies. I was kind of leery of this not just because of drowning but also because I had taken off my ammo belt to keep it dry. So I only had the one magazine in my M16. Eighteen rounds of ammunition across a river all by your self is not much if you encountered the enemy. (Especially, when one of my biggest fears was of getting captured.) Well, I didn't encounter the enemy but I did go in over my head. As they were pulling me back I tried to keep my rifle above the water as best I could. Just when I was ready to drop my rifle and start swimming they managed to pull me back to a shallower spot. I went over my head two or three more times and my rifle went under water twice so they brought me dry rifles as replacements so I could proceed. Finally I made it to the other side, tied off the rope and the rest of the platoon and company made the crossing.

When Pete Milner from our squad got across the river he started screaming. He had ripped the crotch out of his fatigues and he had 6 leeches on his groin area. We had mosquito repellent, which worked better at taking leeches off than repelling mosquitoes, but it also burned. Pete and the medic finally got the leeches off him but I have never heard someone swear such a sustained blue streak in all my life. At the end of his tirade, he said 'Oh God, how I hate this place.' And this pretty much summed up how all of us felt. Guys would write a saying on their helmets—'When I die I'll go to heaven because I've already been in hell—Vietnam'....

Pete Milner and I became good friends. Pete was from Topeka Kansas. Pete was a likeable guy but he sure hated Vietnam and the war we were fighting. He was a 'sad sack' kind of a guy often complaining about something—leeches, mosquitoes, heat, rain, you name it. But Pete played basketball in high school, like me, so I liked him as we had a lot in common.

5 O'clock Sniper
Oct '68

After the river crossing we continued operating in the lowlands whose terrain was marked by rice paddies, villages and a fair amount of small trees—not jungle. There were numerous paths through the trees and we set up a perimeter at the edge of the trees and ran patrols out of this perimeter for the next week or so. We had our patrols return to the perimeter by late afternoon to allow time to eat and set up the guard schedule before dark. At the end of the first day of patrols it was 5:00pm when we heard rounds being fired. We first thought they were mortar rounds but as they hit us it became obvious these were grenades—likely from a G.I. issue M79 grenade launcher. A sniper was firing at us with one of our own weapons. These grenades would explode on impact which often was up in the trees around our perimeter—showering us with shrapnel. That first time we had two or three guys wounded as we had foxholes but had not covered them with logs and sandbags. I got a small piece of shrapnel in my arm as I had my arms up covering my head during the attack. It was very superficial. It burned but did not bleed as it must have cauterized the blood vessels. I didn't even mention it as it was nothing—especially compared to the other casualties. The sniper was some distance off so we could not spot him or return fire as he lobbed the grenades in on us.

The next day, again at 5:00 o'clock, the sniper lobbed another set of grenades in on us—seemingly from the same area. We took a couple more casualties as this was getting old. We decided to try to ambush this guy so we had a fire-team go out before dawn and find a hiding place in the area where we thought the sniper was firing from. They hid all day until 5:00 when the sniper opened up again. Our guys were not too close to him but they saw him and gave chase. It turned out this was kind of a papa-son VC as he was older—maybe in his 40's. Our fire-team consisting of three guys, all about 20 years old, had no trouble running him down. He had one grenade left but he shot that wildly and was no match for our guys with their M16's. We never knew exactly where he came from but he was dead and we had our M79 back....

Tigers & Body Counts
Nov 68

On one of our next stand downs the first night on perimeter guard duty we heard movement out in front by the constatina (barbed) wire. I got on the radio and requested the search light be shown in front of our position. We couldn't believe our eyes as we saw a Bengal tiger sitting just outside the wire looking at us. One of the guys raised his rifle and was going to shoot the tiger. But I said wait and I got on the radio and requested permission to blow up the tiger. The guy on the radio said 'roger that—hold on' as he needed to check with the officer in charge. He got back on the radio and said 'negative you cannot blow up the tiger'. I said 'what are we supposed to do?' He said 'hold on' and then he came back and said 'throw a rock at it and see what happens'. I said 'roger that but if he jumps the wire and comes after us we're going to blow him up'. So we threw a rock at the tiger and he ran back into the jungle. No tiger skin rug for us—as if we needed one.

A day later they told our platoon that we had to go out and do a body count. Apparently they had caught a company of NVA out in the open and our Cobra Guns ships had cleaned up on them. We were moaning and groaning and started packing up our stuff. They said we would only be out a couple of hours so all we needed were our helmets, rifles, ammo belts and a canteen. So we went out on Hueys and they dropped us off. We searched the area and found a lot of blood trails but no bodies. They told us to widen our search and finally we requested they send choppers out to pick us up. They said negative—we had to stay out all night with no gear—no nothing. It was like it was our fault there was no big body count—which I am sure they wanted. We couldn't believe it. Without our ponchos and camouflage blankets we had no protection against rain or mosquitoes. And we got both that night. It was absolutely miserable. First the mosquitoes came and then the rain. (I ended up with two different types of malaria and I'd be willing to bet I caught them that night.) Finally it was morning and we figured they would finally send out the choppers but no they wanted us to look for some more bodies or kill some enemy and count the bodies or whatever. And, of course, at the end of he day we were not going back in but they were sending our stuff out on choppers.

When we got our stuff it was hard to find your own gear and once we did we couldn't believe it. The low life guys who put our stuff on the choppers apparently took time to go through our stuff and steal what they wanted. I lost a new carton of Marlboros and my favorite machete. If we knew who the guys were that stole our stuff we would have messed them up good. The rest of the company finally got done with their stand-down and joined us out in the field about 2 days later. When we set up our perimeter that night, after they joined us, I took my M16 and went to every fox hole looking for my machete but really looking for the guy who had it. There was a lot of talk about Butler walking around half crazy looking for the guy who took his machete. Thank God I never found him because he had messed with the wrong guy. You don't steal a machete from a point man. In fact, if you value your life, you don't mess with a point man—period.

The 'Infamous Machete'

Bad Things
Nov 68

One of the guys in our squad carried our M79 grenade launcher. His nickname was Kid (I never knew his real name— just Kid). Occasionally Kid would walk point with his M79. Normally he would have a grenade round loaded into his M79 but when on point he used a canister round which was like a super powerful shot gun shell. He was on point as we had moved into a wooded area with some small hills. Word came back that we were tracking a small group of NVA along a path. All of a sudden we heard a loud single shot. Kid had turned a corner on a narrow path and had run straight into an NVA soldier. Kid shot him in the face which knocked him down but didn't kill him. The next guy behind came forward and got there just as the NVA was starting to get up. Our guy killed him with his machete—nearly hacking his head off. As we proceeded up the path, the body was right by the path and everyone took turns kicking the corpse in the head as we walked by. No-one told us to do it but everyone did.

A few weeks later two other strange things happened. First of all word came back to me that our point man was smoking pot. Guys smoking pot back at base camp was one thing but not out in the field and for sure never on point. Well, I was a fire team leader so I had to do something. I walked forward and found our point man and just as I was told, he was smoking a joint. I told him to put it out and that he couldn't smoke pot and walk point. He was kind of high and said 'who's going to make me' and I said 'I was' as I snapped the safety off my M-16. He looked at me and laughed. He flipped his joint at me and said 'I like you Butler, you've got guts'. I could have turned him in, but mostly we dealt with our own. Later that day we came upon a freshly dug grave. We were given orders to dig it up and see what was in it. So one of the guys dug up the grave and found an NVA corpse that probably had been dead for a week. The smell was horrendous but it didn't seem to bother this guy as he proceeded to cut the corpse's heart out with his bayonet. After doing this he stunk so much after that you could smell him about 5 feet away. And it was another three weeks or so before we went back to the rear area where we showered and got clean fatigues. Again, I could have turned the guy in for mutilating a corpse but like I said we dealt with our own and in the big scheme of things this was nothing, strange but nothing.

A couple of days later we had point again and I was walking point. We were still in the lowland with the more typical terrains of tree lines, hedge rows and rice paddies. I had just left a tree line and was crossing a rice paddy when a sniper opened up on me. I took cover behind a dike and the firing stopped. After a bit, my fire team linked up with me but as they came out into the open this time at least two snipers opened up with automatic weapons. We returned fire into the tree-line across from the rice paddies. Again the firing finally stopped. Then the rest of our squad linked up—this time without enemy fire. Our squad leader, C.S., was a corporal who had been in the Army for over 15 years and had been busted (reduced in rank) numerous times. He told me to take my fire team across the rice paddy and check out the tree-line where the snipers had been. I said 'What!—You want me to take my men out in the open across the rice paddy—directly in the enemy's line of fire. He said 'Yes, I know Charlie he hits and runs—they'll be gone' I said how about if I take my fire team back into our tree line and follow the tree line around and come up behind them. He said no—he wanted us to go across the rice paddy. I said no. He said that he was giving me a direct order to go and if I disobeyed a direct order in combat I would be court-martialed. I again said no but offered again to take my men around the tree-line. C.S. said no & he would send my men across the rice paddies. I said he couldn't send me or my men across the rice paddies into the enemy's line of fire. He told me to stay where I was and I was under arrest. He then called on the radio for the rest of our platoon to link up. Once they were out in the open, close to us, 2 or 3 snipers opened up on us again from the same area. I got in C.S's face and said 'you dumb shit, you would have gotten all of us killed—now lets see who's gonna get court martialled.' He never said another word about any of that. Technically I suppose I still could have been court martialled but nothing was done. This was probably the biggest/toughest decision I have made in my life. If I would have followed the order we would have been killed or at least severely wounded. If I would have been wrong and the snipers had left, I would have been court martialled which likely would have put me in prison, given me a dishonorable discharge and ruined my life. No-one should have to make those kinds of decisions—least of all a 19 year old kid. And I can tell you that decision has affected me throughout my life. Every time I am told to do something that doesn't make sense, I bristle because I know the consequences can be very great, indeed.

CHAPTER 8

▼

TOO GOOD, TOO FAST AND CARELESS

Now it was the September/October time period. Our company continued conducting search and destroy missions. When we were attached to the tanks, certain of the tanks had flame throwers. Some of our search and destroy missions called for us to destroy entire villages which were know to be V.C. strong holds. When we encountered these villages, again, the men were always gone so we'd round up the women and children and move them out of the village. Then the flame thrower tanks would go through and burn the villages down. The villages consisted of grass huts which burnt very easily and completely. We didn't seem to care about the women and children who now had no where to live. This may seem harsh but at a minimum they were V.C. sympathizers if not V.C. themselves. Many booby traps were set by women and children. So I guess they were lucky we just didn't kill them, which we had been tempted many times to do.

Milner's M60
Nov 68

On one mission we were in the very beginning of the highlands. The terrain was characterized by small hills with some trees and elephant grass but no jungle. I recall after one C.A. we set up our perimeter on one hill. Some of the gun ships had received return fire from another hill during the operation. The gun ships had returned to our fire support base for refueling and more ammo and they came back. We watched as these gun ships made pass after pass over this one hill, mini-guns blazing and still there was return fire. This continued into dusk and we could clearly see the tracer rounds from the gun ships and return fire tracers from the enemy and their AK47s. I remember thinking how tough this enemy was to be shooting back at Cobra gun ships with their small arms. Eventually the firing stopped and the next day we went to that hill. The enemy was gone and so were their dead as evidenced by more blood trails.

Given the enemy activity in the area we decided to maintain our same perimeter and to run patrols out from that perimeter. One day our platoon was preparing to go out on patrol and we were deciding who got to stay back and guard the perimeter. Our M60 machine gunner (the leaches on the groin guy), Pete Milner, was bitching because he never got to stay back because we always had to have the M60 on patrol. I told him to give me his f.... gun and I would take it and he could stay back. He said OK, and maybe even thanks. But he warned me not to fire it unless I absolutely had to because it was a big pain in the ass to clean. I said OK and we set out. We were patrolling in some rocky hills with tree cover. We encountered the enemy and a small fire fight commenced but did not last long. I set up the M60 on some big high rocks overlooking an opening not far from where the enemy shooting was coming from. Some of our guys advanced on the enemy position and about 5 NVA come running out of the tree line into our opening. I began firing the M60 and was walking the machine gun rounds right up to them when my gun jammed. I looked down and saw my foot was on the ammunition belt causing the gun to jam. I opened up the gun, cleared it and was going to recommence firing but the NVA were gone. I don't know if they had any idea how close they were to being killed because I had them dead to rights. I guess it wasn't meant to be. When we returned to our perimeter, Milner had heard his M60 being fired and asked if I got any kills. I said no they weren't in the open long enough to zero in on them. I failed to mention stepping on the ammo belt. So Milner was pissed because he had to clean his gun. What he didn't know is he would have had 5 kills had he been there. I felt guilty about screwing up with my foot on the ammo belt. But someone said 'yea Miller probably would have gotten them, but the ammo bearer had the responsibility of making sure you had a clear feed from the gun to the ammo belt can which he did not do'. Whatever, I still felt I screwed up.

Pete Milner

Jungle Surprises
Dec 68

As we moved back into the highlands and the jungle it never ceased to amaze us that no matter how long you had been in the jungle almost everyday you saw something new, unusual and often terrifying. We had already encountered triple canopies, bamboo forests, two step snakes, komodo dragons, leeches, huge spiders, iridescent jungle flora, malaria laden mosquitoes, elephant grass and a host of other things. So you would think we had seen most of what the jungle had to offer. Not so. Within the next week's time we came across many new surprises the jungle had in store for us.

There were these animals up in the trees that looked like huge bobcats with bushy tails like squirrels. When we encountered them they were in the trees and all over the place. They were probably fifty to seventy-five feet above our heads as they jumped from tree to tree. They didn't make any noise but it was disconcerting to say the least to have these big cats jumping around over our heads as we proceeded through the jungle.

We also encountered some new and bigger snakes. We found a big python that someone had apparently killed. It looked like it had been stabbed and then shot in the head. This was the biggest snake I had ever seen and it was chilling to think these things were around as we trudged through the jungles and slept on the jungle floor at night. But this wasn't going to be the biggest snake we encountered. A few days later we came across a huge yellow/green snake that was dead and was hanging out of a tree next to the narrow path we were on. This snake was about a foot in diameter and seemed to be twenty to thirty feet long. I remember at the time not knowing what this was and wondering why someone threw it up in a tree. Afterward we came to realize that this was an anaconda that often would go up into trees and then drop down on their prey. I remember walking way too close to this monster snake as we passed it on our path. It sure looked dead but we hoped it wasn't faking as we passed within a foot or so of it.

And you would think this anaconda was the largest animal we would encounter in the jungle. Not so again. We were sleeping in our hooches one morning and just at dawn we were awakened by some thunderous crashing sounds coming toward us in the jungle. Just as we were coming out of our little hooches three or four elephants came crashing through our perimeter as if they were being stampeded. Some guys barely had gotten out of their hooches when they were flattened during the stampede. We had heard that sometimes the NVA would use them to carry heavy weapons and supplies. We didn't see anything on these elephants so we never figured out where they came from or what they were all about. We just wrote them off as another jungle surprise.

Montagnards

The only people that lived in the jungles of the central highlands of Vietnam were a primitive tribal group known as the 'Montagnards'. They were native to these jungles in Vietnam and had been converted to Christianity probably by some missionaries at some point. These people wore loin clothes and no tops—not even the women which of course caught the attention of us G.I.'s. These people were sympathetic and helpful to us Americans as we were viewed as Christians helping to fight off the heathen communists of the north. Some of the Montagnards were used as scouts by certain American combat units but not us. At one point we came upon a village. They had prepared food and offered us some. One of the dishes were very little birds which they had cooked. Similar birds were flying around up in the trees of the jungle. And they showed us how they shot them down with their very small cross-bows. And they were so accurate with these cross-bows they shot these small birds down in flight. It was unbelievable.

So, occasionally we encountered some of their primitive small villages but mostly they were a mystery to us. We knew they were not Viet Cong or NVA so we pretty much left them alone.

Jungle Rot/Monsoons/Typhoon/Caps (not taps)
Dec 68

As we continued though these jungles they became thicker and seemed to have an inordinate number of sharp vines and thorns that would cut up your hands and arms as you hacked your ways through the jungle on point. I had jungle rot real bad on my hands. When I woke up in the mornings and moved my hands, puss would come out of the jungle rot sores. Mine was bad but Mike Leeks had it worse as he and I were walking a lot of point. After one particularly bad point day for Mike he was showing me his hands and arms. They were all cut up and full of pussy jungle rot. He told me they hurt like mad. The medic was giving us some kind of pills to help the stuff. Apparently Mike took too many pills one night because his houch (mini-tent) was next to mine and he went into convulsions. I got the medic and we had to pry his mouth open and dig out his tongue because he was choking on it. I used a canteen cup handle to pry his teeth open. In doing this we chipped one of his front teeth but were able to get him breathing again. He was half unconscious all night and was in real bad shape come morning. We called in a medivac helicopter to take him to the hospital. Mike was awake but kind of delirious as the chopper sat down. He started running toward it and fell down, his ruc sack coming up over his head. I went and put his arm over my shoulder and was walking him to the chopper. But he kept falling down. Finally I picked him up and put him over my shoulder, carried him to the chopper and kind of threw him in. The medic started attending to him as they took off. We didn't see Mike again for a month or so during which time he was in the hospital trying to clear up his jungle rot and whatever else had put him into convulsions. I'll never forget how pathetic Mike looked trying to get to that chopper.

Later the Hollies (a rock band) came out with the song 'He's Not Heavy, He's My Brother'. And to this day, I always think of carrying Mike and putting him on the chopper when I hear that song. We were all like brothers, but especially Mike—he and I were very close. And on that day in the God forsaken jungles of Vietnam, when I put him over my shoulder and carried him—he wasn't heavy he was my brother.

Mike Leeks

With the advent of November came the rain. November and December was monsoon season in Vietnam. It rained and rained and rained. Weeks would go by with constant rain. Each night we would build our little hooches from our ponchos.

We'd crawl under them to sleep and the warmth of our bodies would dry out our jungle fatigues by morning. But every morning they would say pack it up. So we'd get out of our hooches in the pouring rain and pack up our gear. We'd be soaking wet again within a couple of minutes. And we would trudge off through the constant rain into the steamy jungles or rice paddies. The only good thing about the monsoons was that it seemed there was little enemy contact during the heavy rains. Maybe it was because of the limited vision or the constant noise of the rain both of which would limit your ability to detect the enemy. I remember, however, a stretch of a week or so where we were making constant contact with the enemy in spite of the rains. Sometimes the contact was during the day and sometimes at night. Normally we would take off our boots and socks at night to allow your feet to dry. But with all the enemy contact I did not take off my boots or socks for over a week. The fear was encountering the enemy with your boots off. Once things had calmed down and I took my boots and socks off, the top layer of skin came off my feet. Our medic put something on it but it burned like mad. They had to call in a medivac as I had emersion foot (called trench foot in earlier wars). I was back in the fire support base for 4 or 5 days to clear up my feet. When I came back to my unit it was still raining and they told us to dig our fox holes very deep as there was a typhoon headed towards us that night. About half way through the night the storm hit us. The rain and wind was ferocious. As we waited the storm out our fox holes filled with water up to our necks. It was miserable but we had little choice due to the wind and flying trees. The next morning the storm subsided but we couldn't believe our eyes. We were on a hill about a mile from the South China Sea. We could clearly see the coast and the sea before the storm.

But after the rains and flooding it was like we were on an island—nothing but water/sea all around us. So they called in helicopters that took us off our island and on to another mission. And it was like—what's going to happen to us next—as if the Viet Cong, NVA, the jungle and everything else were not enough.

Only a week or so later we had set up our perimeter for the night and I was eating some c-rations when something kind of stuck in my throat. I coughed it out and it was a dental cap from one of my front teeth on the bottom. Some how it had come off even though I had not been eating an apple or anything like that. Well, this was a problem as my tooth under the cap is a spike with the nerve exposed. It hurt like mad so I went to the medic. He didn't have any dental cement or anything else to fix it so he said I would have to go back to the rear on the next chopper. So that is what I did and the medics at the medical tent at our fire support base didn't have any ability to fix this either. They sent me to Quinn Ohn where they had a hospital and larger medical facility, and a dentist. The dentist told me I was lucky I still had the cap. Otherwise they would have had to send me to Japan to have a new cap made. And I found out that if they send you to Japan with less than 4 months to go in Vietnam, you don't go back to Vietnam—you go home. This was December and I had less than 4 months. I wished so much I would have swallowed that cap or otherwise lost it. But the cement held and I went back to the field.

CHAPTER 9

▼

NUMB, DON'T CARE

Finally in December the rains became less constant and it started clearing up. But I was becoming numb. Maybe it was from seeing so many of my buddies get hurt or killed—many times while on point. I was convinced I would never leave Vietnam in one piece and more likely dead. It was like it was bound to happen so it might as well happen sooner than later. I didn't necessarily want to get killed but I was fried. I didn't really care about myself anymore. I cared far more about my buddies. In fact I became so convinced I wasn't coming home I wrote my fiancée, Judy, and told her to call off the wedding because there wasn't any point—I wouldn't make it home anyway.

Pungi Pit/Mike is Wounded
Dec 68

We were back in the lowlands. There were some rice paddies but a lot of trees and paths through the forests. Normally we tried to avoid paths especially in the jungle. But if they were more in the open it was easier to see any bobby traps, etc. Well, I was on point again and I was proceeding on a path that ran along a tree-line and next to a number of rice paddies. As I was walking I saw soldiers far across two or three rice paddies. They were far enough away that I couldn't tell if they were Americans or NVA. We had not been told of other American units in the area but my experience was we were often not told things we should have been told. I continued walking as I looked intently at the other soldiers trying to identify them. When all of a sudden I fell into a deep hole. I knew what had happened before I hit the ground—I had fallen into a pungi pit. I landed on my back and I thought I was dead. My buddies came running up and asked if I was OK. I looked down at myself, expecting to see bamboo stakes sticking out of my chest but there were none. It took me a minute to answer because the wind was knocked out of me. I said I thought I was OK and I slowly got up and they helped me out. Then they showed me the other pit next to the one I had fallen into—it was full of pungi stakes. They said I was lucky to have fallen into the right one. I wasn't so sure about that. I wanted it over. And, of course, the other soldiers across the rice paddies turned out to be another American unit that we had not been told about.

Finally, after a few weeks Mike Leeks came back to our platoon. But Mike was destined to run into trouble. On one of the first few nights after Mike was back we were hit in the middle of the night by a group of VC. There was a tremendous amount of AK47 fire and I could hear the rounds cracking as they went right over my head, shredding my poncho. I turned over and low-crawled head first into my fox hole—right on top of Mike Leeks. After I got off him he said he had been hit. I lit my cigarette lighter in the fox-hole and saw Mike's face covered in blood. The shooting had quieted down now following a couple of big explosions. I yelled for the medic and as it turned out, Mike had been grazed by an AK47 round that creased his eyebrow. He was very lucky and was sent back to the rear area again via medivac. And the explosions I had heard were a couple of our claymore mines that we had fired at the enemy and had killed two of them. The battalion commander came out to our unit and he saw the dead VC. He was not happy because some of our guys had cut the VC's ears off and pressed jump wings into their foreheads. I never did things like this but some guys had necklaces of human ears. As far as the jump wings in the forehead, the guys thought they would send a message to the enemy that this is what happens when you mess with the 173d. This may sound horrible to the reader but far worse things happen in war than mutilation of the dead. War is horrible and horrible things happen. This was just a little part of it....

The Longest Night/Too Much
Dec 68—Mar 69

After the last mission we came back to our fire support base for a stand-down. As soon as we got there word came down 'guess who just got here'. It was one of the drill sergeants from jump school. All of the drill sergeants were SOBs but this guy was the worst. Not only would he insult you but he would say horrible things about your mother or your girl friend. Well, there was a lot of talk about how long he would make it here in Vietnam. Well, the answer was two nights. On his second night someone rolled a grenade in his sleeping quarters and he was killed. I don't know who did this but no-one was upset about it. Many thought this guy got what he deserved.

After the third day of our stand-down they woke us up in the middle of the night and told us we had to walk point out of the base camp at night down the highway. This was very scary because we never moved at night. Our platoon had point so I said 'f … it' I'll do point—don't mean nothin. So here I was walking down the middle of the highway at night. We were told to cross some rice paddies and then cross an old railroad trestle. Just on the other side of the trestle we got hit. Machine gun fire, rockets, and mortars—the whole works. We were pinned down behind a rice paddy dike and it continued. We started firing back and were told to stop because it was ARVN's (Army of the Republic of Vietnam—they were South Vietnamese soldiers) that had us pinned down by mistake. It was the longest night of my life. We were pinned down for about 4 to 5 hours. You could see the tracer rounds (from M16's and M60 machine guns) flying over you—just above your head. And when they fired rockets it looked like the 4th of July except these also came much too close as they passed over our heads. At one point they started walking the mortar rounds in on us. You could hear them whistling in and the ground would shake as each mortar round hit. They were getting closer and closer. Not only was the ground shaking but we were coming up off the ground as the shells hit very near to us. I was very scared this time. Actually I was terrified, nearly scared to death, as I thought for sure this was it. And all of a sudden I wasn't scared anymore. It was like God put his hand on my shoulder and calmed me. I saw all of the people I loved flash before my eyes—my fiancé, Judy, my Mom, my Dad, my sisters, Bev and Bonnie and my brother, Ken. Also there were two of my very favorite people—my dead grandfather, Earl and my dead little league coach Big Bill. They were smiling and I knew this was the end and God was taking me. But it never happened. The RVN's mortar tube was rusty and had never been cranked up that far to shoot rounds that close and they couldn't quite get us. And then finally at dawn our tanks came and we were saved. But a big part of me died that night. I know I was never the same after that. I got more and more numb and didn't care about anything. It was like I was in a daze. I felt like a walking zombie. Sometimes after a big firefight it was not uncommon to feel dazed for a while. Often wondering how in the world you had survived. But this was different. This daze did not go away. I remember still feeling it days later and thinking I had gone crazy.

And the next time I walked point I walked straight into an NVA base camp without ever seeing it. One of my buddies tackled me right before the shooting started. After it was over they asked me what was wrong. Why did I keep going? I said I never saw anything—even though the signs were clearly there—so obvious. I was fried. The medic told me to get on a helicopter and go back to base camp. I was then diagnosed with combat fatigue and was taken out of combat for the rest of my tour (mid January to March). I remember feeling very guilty about not being out in combat with my buddies. But I knew I was done. I had walked point too many times and point had gotten the best of me....

Too Much

Mike's Farewell
Mar '69

At the end Mike was reassigned to the fire-support base as well. Point had taken its toll on Mike, too. I remember the wild/crazy look Mike had gotten in his eyes. Mike and I got to spend about a month together at the fire support base before he went home. Mike and I became very close as our experiences were nearly identical. Mike's dad owned a sporting good store so when Mike got packages from home he got all kinds of things including a pearl handled 45 caliber pistol. It had a holster with bullets all around the waist band and a tie down on the leg. Mike looked like a cowboy when he wore it. On the day he left to go home he gave me his 45 and holster. That was the last time I saw him and he was going home with that wild look in his eyes—no longer a kid but as a fried point man.

Mike's Farewell

Pete Milner had enough too. He extended his tour (after 9 months) in Vietnam by 6 months so he could go home early on a 30 day leave. He would have 8 more months to go when he got back from his leave but he had extended to be a guard on the perimeter of Ahn Khe. But the Army and Vietnam got Pete as well. After his leave he found out the perimeter guard duty had been transferred to the RVNS (South Vietnamese Army). So they sent Pete back out to our Company in combat. Pete later stepped on a booby trap and blew his foot off. I never saw or heard from Pete Milner again. We went our separate ways after Vietnam. I don't know if Pete went to college after the service but I suspect he did as he was a sharp guy. One thing I'll bet he didn't do in college was play basketball—with only one foot …

Pete Milner was done too

The Last Few Weeks
Mar—Apr '69

When I had about twenty days left, I developed this tremendous sore throat. It got so bad I couldn't eat or drink and I had a fever. I went to the medical tent and they gave me some antibiotics but the next day it was worse and I still couldn't eat or drink anything. They sent me to see an ear nose and throat specialist at the hospital in Quinn Ohn. He checked me and said I had an acute case of tonsillitis and he was going to put me in the hospital. In the hospital I would get an IV for intravenous feedings and antibiotics. So they put me in a ward where 95% of the patients had been wounded. I remember waking up in the middle of the night and my arm was killing me. I started yelling for a nurse who finally came after I had awakened most of the ward. I had had a nightmare about the war and my tossing and turning had caused the needle to come out of the vein and to swell up under my skin. The nurse was not happy about this as she had to redo the IV. This time they jammed part of the tube up inside my vein and secured the whole thing with some kind of a board. I told them it didn't feel very good and they said too bad. The next morning the Chaplin came by and was stopping by talking and encouraging the wounded soldiers. At that point I could barely talk so he asked where I had been hit and I motioned to my throat. He came closer and was looking at my throat and I managed to squeak out 'tonsilitis'. He promptly walked away and on to the next soldier apparently looking for more serious wounds/conditions than tonsillitis. I was embarrassed to say the least. Later in the day I was starting to feel better and the nurse told me I could get up and walk to the bathroom holding my IV bottle up high. Once in the bathroom she showed me the hook for me to hang the bottle on as she warned me not to get the bottle too low as it would back-up. So I commenced to get up, go to the bathroom and come back to bed. Somehow I had managed to get the bottle too low and blood had backed up into the bottle. I knew I was in trouble but I thought if I hung it back up it would just run back into me and maybe be done before the nurse noticed. No such luck. The nurse came by and she said' you got the bottle too low didn't you?' I said' no I think it just kind of backed up all by itself.' She didn't say a word as she walked away. But when she came back she had a bedpan and I guess I kind of knew I'd been had.

Well the next day I was feeling better and was able to eat and drink again. The Dr came by and said I was well and he was sending me to Japan to get my tonsils out. I got very excited because I knew I would not come back to Vietnam. The Dr. asked me why I was so excited and I told him I only had 16 days left. He said in that case he would not send me to Japan and I should get my tonsils out back in the states and discharged me (and I still have my tonsils to this day). When the nurse came by to take out my IV she said something like "looks like you get to go back to your unit trooper". She knew a paratroop unit was nowhere near as nice as her hospital duty in Quinn Ohn. I said "not for long I've only got 16 days left. How many do you have"? She just pointed to the door and said "get dressed and get out". Too bad but that nurse just didn't seem to have any sense of humor.

After I got back from the hospital and had about two weeks left I decided to go to the PX at Phu Cat Air Force base. It was down Highway 1 and you could catch rides on army trucks to get there. So with Mike's 45 strapped to my leg off I went by myself. The trip down there was uneventful so I went to the PX and got some cigarettes and some other stuff and then looked for a ride back to LZ Uplift—our fire support base. The only truck I could find going my way was RVN's so I jumped aboard. About half way back to Uplift the truck turned off and started down another road which was not the way to Uplift. I told them to stop and asked if they could take me to Uplift? They said no so I got out at the crossroads. There were no trucks or anything on the highway so I started getting nervous standing out there all alone with my 45. There was a little shack at the crossroads where you could buy cokes, whores and who knew what else. So I got a coke and sat down on the small porch in the shade—waiting for a ride to come along. All of a sudden the air force military police came roaring up in jeep. Some guys who had been with whores in the back room ran out the back. A couple of us sitting on the porch just sat there. The MP's told us this place was off limits and they were going to give us DR's (disciplinary reports). I was the only NCO (non-commissioned officer) so I told the MP's to go after the guys running out the back who had been messing with the whores. But they didn't seem to want to listen as I got a DR just for sitting there drinking a coke. I told them it wasn't safe at the crossroads by myself, but to no avail. They did, however, give me a ride to uplift. And I guess I had the last laugh as that DR never caught up with me. Maybe a supervisor read it and thought it was ridiculous and tore it up. Or, more likely, it got lost between the Air Force and the Army somewhere between Vietnam and the states.

A few days after my DR our 1st sergeant (top) asked me to take another guy from our company as a replacement for Mike Leaks. I told top I was concerned because the guy was a total screw-up. Top asked me to give him a try so I did. After about 2 days I told him to do something and he said no—'who's going to make me?' I said 'I was because I was a sergeant and he was a PFC (private first class). He then grabbed his M16, locked and loaded (chambered a round), took the safety off and pointed it at me and said 'now who's going to make me?' I told him to put it down right now and nothing would happen to him. He started crying and said he was going to kill me. After a couple of minutes I got him to give me his M16. I took it, pointed it at him and marched him down to the 1st sergeant. Top said he would take care of it and I never saw the guy again.

And finally with 10 days to go, I was in my tent sleeping when we were attacked. We could hear the mortar rounds whistling in and exploding all around so I got up quick and headed out of my tent to our bunker which was only about 10 yards from the tent. At that point I was by myself and I heard AK47 fire and I got concerned that we were being over-run. In my haste I had not brought my rifle with me into the bunker. I decided I better go get it. As I found my M16 and was heading back to the bunker an enemy rocket was fired and it hit right in front of me. The concussion knocked me down and almost out. In a daze I crawled into the bunker. A couple of guys were now in the bunker and one of them kept saying we "we're getting over ran (by the enemy) and I have 20 days and I'm going to die". He said this over and over and finally I said "I have 10 days so shut up". But my luck held and as it turned out we were not over run and finally the mortars and rockets quit.

CHAPTER 10

▼

GOING HOME

The Nightmare Ends
Apr '69

Finally it was time for me to go home. I took a military hop on a C130 from Ahn Khe to Cam Rahn Bay where I would be sent home. Part way through the flight we heard a loud snap and the airplane shuddered. Once the plane seemed stable the co-pilot came back and told us they had snapped a steering cable but it was the one that controlled left to right direction. He said they thought they could steer the plane with their propellers—one faster than the other to turn. I thought great after all we'd been through we were going to crash and die on the way home. We continued to hear a 'bang, bang, bang' for the rest of the flight as the steering cable was hitting the side of the aircraft. This was a constant reminder our one last horror of Vietnam. But we landed on a runway lined with emergency vehicles in Cam Rahn Bay without incident. A few days later we were on a commercial jet and I remember clearly the yell that went up in the plane as we lifted off the ground in Vietnam. It was a feeling like God had given me reprieve and I was returning from

Hell—unbelievable. Some guys yelled and a few of us cried. I first yelled—feeling exhilaration beyond belief and then I cried—feeling overwhelmed that this living nightmare was finally over. I had made it. Once we landed in Seattle/Tacoma airport they transported us to Fort Lewis, Washington where they gave us a shower, a steak dinner, new dress uniforms and took us to the airport. I remember my plane landing in Chicago and taxiing to the gate. Judy, her dad and my family were there. We laughed and cried. Judy and I were married 11 days later. I remember very little of my wedding. I was in shell shock....

No Welcome Home/Nightmares/Malaria
Apr '69—Jun '70

When I first came home from Vietnam I learned very quickly not to tell people that I was a Vietnam veteran. There were far too many people who were not only against the war but against the war veterans as well. I'm not sure why but the media portrayed many of us as being crazed baby killers. Well, the crazed part of it was not far off but baby killers? Not hardly. I'm sure a handful of guys snapped and earned that label but most of us were young kids fighting for our country and doing the best we could.

In many ways I was fortunate to have had almost a year and a half to serve following Vietnam. My wife, Judy, and I were stationed at Fort Knox, Kentucky. The military environment was a good place for me. I was a nervous wreck. Some of the guys I got to know told me later that when I first arrived at Fort Knox I was like a basket case. They had never seen anyone so nervous and obviously affected by the war.

My nightmares started almost immediately when I returned. My wife, Judy, can tell you how bad they were. A couple of times I awoke to Judy screaming as I had been choking her and hitting her as I dreamed of hand to hand combat in Vietnam. And she would also tell you one of the scariest things was the way I would go off by myself and sit in a chair and look through my Vietnam pictures for hours on end. I was stuck back in Vietnam.

I also came down with malaria at Fort Knox. I remember not feeling well thinking I had a cold. It was August and I came home from work and laid down on the couch with my fatigues on and I asked Judy for my field jacket as I was cold. It was about 90 degrees that day, we had no air conditioning and I was lying on the couch shivering. Judy had made my favorite dinner—fried chicken and I wasn't hungry. Judy got our neighbor who also had been in Vietnam. He took one look at me and said we were going to the hospital because I had malaria. I told him I did not because I hadn't had it in Vietnam and couldn't have it now. I refused to go to the hospital but he said either I go with him or he was calling an ambulance. So I went to the hospital and had the dubious distinction of being the first case of malaria ever diagnosed at the hospital in Fort Knox. I remember numerous doctors coming by to see me as they had never seen a malaria patient before. I had two of the three different types of malaria and my fever was so high I was having hallucinations and the nurses and Doctors were very concerned. But finally I got better after spending two weeks in the hospital and then had a 45 day convalescent leave

I got an early out from the Army to go to college at the University of Minnesota, Duluth. Prior to applying at UMD I asked the Army (a mistake) if I would be considered a resident of any state upon my discharge given I had no state residency for the past 3 years. They said yes and I would pay in state, not out of state tuition. My first visit to UMD told me otherwise and for the first year I had to pay out of state tuition (3 times that of a resident). Welcome home Vietnam veteran....

CHAPTER 11

▼

PTSD (POST TRAUMATIC STRESS DISORDER)

May '78 to Present

I graduated from college and was doing very well in my career. I had seemingly put Vietnam and my combat fatigue behind me. But about 10 years after Vietnam all of that started to change. My wife and I were having difficulties with our marriage and were seeing counselors (a husband and wife). After a few sessions they called me aside and said they weren't experts but felt I might be suffering from PTSD. They suggested that I go to the Vet Center to get treatment—which I ultimately did. About that same time I remember very clearly washing my car in the driveway and listening to the radio. I heard a helicopter fly over and it sounded very much like a Huey which gave me the chills due to the large number of combat assaults we did with Hueys in Vietnam. At that same time a news report came over the radio announcing that China was staging a number of troops along their border with Vietnam for a possible invasion. China and Vietnam were having border clashes at the time. I got this very strange feeling about wanting to become a mercenary and go fight Vietnam again, this time with China. This feeling became a very strong urge which I knew wasn't right but I could not help my feelings. I started thinking more and more about Vietnam. I was also having trouble with my boss at work. He was messing in my stuff, trying to tell me to do things that didn't make sense and I did not like that.

Post Traumatic Stress

When I went to the Vet Center they hooked me up with a psychiatrist who would talk with me to determine if I had PTSD and what to do about it. I was concerned when I found out this guy had never been to Vietnam, never been in combat or even in the service. I couldn't imagine how such a person could understand my problems related to Vietnam. His name was Jerry, and he asked me what bothered me most about Vietnam. No one had ever asked me that question before. I thought about it for a while and I told him that many of my friends were wounded or killed including one of my best friends, Ray Garza who was killed with 16 days left. I felt guilty about surviving and felt a part of me died in Vietnam. I had trouble relating to people since my return. My definition of friendship changed in Vietnam. Real friends were guys who were willing to die for you if need be and would do almost anything including walking point. My current friends seemed superficial. Most of the things I was doing seemed unimportant. We had a saying in Vietnam—'it don't mean nothing'. Which meant if it wasn't life or death it really didn't matter? I felt like my whole life didn't mean nothing. I felt no one cared about what I did in Vietnam.

I felt abandoned and alone. And that no-one could help me. My psychiatrist, Jerry, listened to me and towards the end tears rolled down his cheeks and he told me I was wrong because he cared about what I did in Vietnam and he would help me. I thought it was strange because psychiatrists were not supposed to cry. But somehow this convinced me that he did understand and he would help. But, I was spiraling down at that point. I had a lot of trouble with my boss—he was messing with me. I remember at one point I told my wife that my boss didn't know who he was messing with. I knew what I would have done to him in Vietnam and I told Judy that he'd better quit messing with me. This scarred Judy, and she told my psychiatrist....

Mike's Death/Bottoming Out

I went through a ton of counseling sessions, including some group therapy. But I was still feeling desperate and all alone. My psychiatrist felt I had unsettled business related to Vietnam especially related to Ray Garza. I had tried to write his Mom from Vietnam about Ray's death but the Army wouldn't give me her address. So I wrote President Reagan (attn Elizabeth Dole) and within a week I got a call from a colonel who said President Reagan had asked him to help me. Ultimately they got a letter forwarded to Ray's mom from me. It came back undeliverable—addressee unknown. At least I had tried. I then decided I needed to contact my other best friend, Mike Leeks. Mike, Ray and I all walked point and I knew if there was any-one I needed to hook up with, it was Mike. I wrote him a letter telling him how much trouble I was having and that I needed to see him. I mailed it to his Mom's address which I still had. I remember very clearly the fall evening I was outside raking leaves and Judy came out and said I had a call from California

& I knew it was Mike. But it wasn't, it was Mike's brother. He said he didn't know how to tell me this but Mike was killed in a hang gliding accident 3 years ago. Mike's brother had been in Vietnam too, as a helicopter pilot. He talked to me for a long time and offered to come to Minneapolis to see me. He said Mike had been having a lot of problems like me before he died. I thanked him but said no. I was crushed—my last hope was gone. It was like being back on point again—all alone but there seemed to be no-one left to link up with me. I almost killed myself. The only reason I didn't was because of my wife and kids. I was even talking to a recruiter thinking that going back in the service might get me closer to people I could relate to. I told Judy that I was scared, all alone and didn't know what to do. I decided I would go talk to a friend of mine, Steve, who had played basketball with me on an over 30 team and was a pastor. I told him I was having psychological problems related to Vietnam and needed to talk to him. I went to his church and we sat down and I told him what was going on and what had happened with Mike. I was crying and I looked up and he was crying. He took me in his arms and we both cried. He said 'I don't know what to say other than to ask God to give you peace, Rick'. And then we held hands and he said the prayer. I can't say that God answered this prayer right away but I knew there were at least two people (beyond my family) that cared what I had done in Vietnam and wanted to help me. And I have thanked God many times for my psychiatrist, Jerry, who saved me. He pulled me up out of a very deep pit. And after two to three years of counseling I not only continued to function but got better....

Mike Leeks—Vietnam ultimately got him too

The Importance of Family

I cannot overly emphasize the importance of my immediate family in helping to cope with PTSD. For me this help started with my fiancée, Judy, still being there when I got home from Vietnam. You don't know how many times I was told, by many different guys in Vietnam, to forget about your girl back home—she won't be there when you return. Well, they were wrong. Judy not only was there but we were married 11 days after I got back from Vietnam. She knew things were not good for me when I got home with my recurring nightmares and then malaria during our time at Fort Knox. My Mom and Dad also knew the war had changed me as they saw many of my struggles after getting back from Vietnam. Having loved ones around

when trying to adjust and put the war behind me was very com-
forting at a very difficult time. Maybe that's why my PTSD
symptoms did not surface in a big way for 10 or 11 years after
my return from Vietnam. And I can tell you that Judy was there
and involved with me and my therapist during many of the sessions we had over the two to three year period I was getting
treatment. And at my worst time I was going to take my life but
the main reason I did not was because of the love I had for Judy
and my two kids, Leslie and Doug. Otherwise I felt I was all
alone. I didn't care about myself anymore but thank God my
family loved me and I cared about them. Judy and I have now
been married almost 38 years. She has helped me immeasurably
in my ability to cope with my PTSD. Encouraging and supporting me throughout my career and personal life. And now Leslie
and Doug are my adult children and they have and continue to
be very supportive as well. Many of the things in this book I
have shared with them over the years. And even some things
that I have chosen not to put in this book. Being able to talk
about the nightmares and memories that haunt me lightens
their burden and helps put them in perspective. I have talked
about Vietnam to every member of my family—not just my
Mom & Dad, but my sisters Bev and Bonnie and my brother,
Ken as well. For all of this love and support not only from my
family but also Judy's family, for all of that, I am eternally grate-
ful. I would not be here today without that.

There is a lot of talk about PTSD today with the returning
combat veterans from the Iraq war. And I have heard it empha-
sized more and more—the importance of family to returning
combat veterans. The chairman of the joint chiefs of staff, Peter
Pace, said 'make no mistake about it, the family of veterans are
serving our country immensely by the burden they gladly bear

in supporting our men and women in uniform—especially those returning combatants with PTSD'.

For many years after my intense counseling, I continued to do well. And in the early 1990's the V.A. (Veteran's Administration) called me in to re-evaluate my PTSD disability that related back to my combat fatigue. I remember going in and was dressed for work in a three piece suit, white shirt & tie—the whole nine yards. The psychiatrist asked me how I was doing and I told him I was cured. I said I was doing fine and didn't want my disability anymore. I told them to take the money and to give it to someone else because I was well. I remember he looked at me kind of funny and said he still had a few questions for me. I can't remember just exactly what his questions were but I know they were about Vietnam and my feelings about certain things. As I was answering his questions everything started flooding back to me. I became overwhelmed and started crying as I talked about the horrors of Vietnam that still haunted me. He said I was not cured and would never get over those experiences. I had just managed to put them in my back pocket and pretend they weren't there. He asked if I wanted to get back into counseling again. I said I didn't think so because the last time I bottomed out so low I almost killed myself. He said it was up to me. But he would not let me give back my disability and gave me his card should I decide to go into counseling again. And I continued to do well—apparently becoming skilled at my 'back pocket' coping mechanism.

Then there was 9/11/01 and we were at war again and there was a lot of focus on the military. I felt a need to talk with veterans about how I was feeling—wanting to re-up but knowing that was unrealistic given my age and my health. There were no vets around at work or at least very few and we were unconnected. I started having some conversations with an electrician who had been with the 1st Infantry Division in Vietnam. But that was it. Want to guess how many Vietnam veterans, let alone combat veterans, are successful business people today? I am quite sure there are very few because I only met a couple of Vietnam Vets in my 30 year business career. So I was feeling very unconnected and alone again—my 'back pocket' was coming unraveled. Then I heard that the 173d Airborne Brigade (my Vietnam unit) had annual reunions and I heard the next one was going to be in Rochester, Mn. I wanted to go but was afraid to go as well. I signed up but was still unsure if this was good for me to do. I did go and looked through a big sign-up sheet of all the guys who were attending & I only saw one name that I recognized Smitty. I knew Smitty—he was a friend, not a close friend, but I knew him. Smitty had walked point a lot and I was there when he was wounded. When I saw him he hugged me and picked me up and told his buddy that I had came and got him that night in the jungles of Vietnam when he got blown up. I was surprised to see how bad he was limping. I remember the night he got hit all too well. Smitty was caught in the ambush during Operation Cochise. I always had felt guilty as I thought maybe it should have been me and my fire team on ambush that night. But I had thought he got his million dollar wound. But I then saw this was anything but a superficial wound. Smitty had almost died and had spent 6 months in the hospital. As Smitty and I talked I told him that after he and his team had gotten ambushed our platoon (Mike Platoon) had been considered 'wiped out' as there were only 7 of us left. So we were disbanded and reassigned to other platoons. Smitty got this terrified look on his face and I asked him what was wrong. He said he had never known that Mike platoon was wiped out.

And that was the second platoon of his that was wiped out. The first one was in the battle of BanMeThout. I felt very bad for Smitty. I realized how lucky Smitty had been—having survived two platoons being wiped out.

I told Smitty about my run-in with C.S. and my refusal to cross the rice paddies with my fire team as C.S. had ordered. I told him how that experience had a big affect on me. And to this day I bristle at things that people ask me to do that don't make sense. I told my psychiatrist that and how I attribute that to my Vietnam experience. She suggested that maybe I was just the kind of person who didn't like being told what to do. I laughed and told her that I had not only been a good soldier but a good paratrooper. And you can't be either one if you do not know when and how to keep your mouth shut and follow orders. So there is a time to shut up and follow orders and there is a time to ask questions and then follow orders. And, sometimes even a time to suffer the consequences of not following orders.

I believe good managers/bosses are OK with and even encourage questions about what is to be done. I also know there are others who do not care to hear anything—just shut up and do it. Towards the end of my business career I had the misfortune of having too many 'shut up and do it' bosses. I became very concerned that the combination of my resurgent PTSD and this 'shut up and do it' attitude was a prescription for big trouble. When people tell me to do something that makes no sense, I get very angry and have flash backs to C.S. giving me orders to cross that rice paddy in Vietnam. My buddy Smitty says he goes to Vietnam every night when he goes to bed. I can't say that's true every night for me. But it's true far too many nights. And as for the nightmares, they are always there just waiting to happen. Not every night or every week. But generally once a month or more as they whisper their Vietnam horrors to me as I sleep.

So I started looking into early retirement as opposed to looking for another job at 55 after my job was eliminated and things were screwed up at work. This made my wife very nervous. I was feeling more and more isolated. I didn't have any real close friends at work. I have some friends but only one best friend left, Marty, in Indiana. I have known Marty all my life and played basketball together in high school. I tried talking to Marty a few times about Vietnam, the things that bothered me, But it was hard for me to explain my feelings and hard for Marty (and others) to understand. But things have changed with Marty now; his son was in the Marine Corps and saw combat in Afghanistan. So Marty knows a lot more about the military now and understands things differently. So we stay in touch and he continues to be my life-long best friend. But he, like many of us, is caught up in the demands of his work, travels a lot and is seldom home. But even when home he is 450 miles from me (Minneapolis to Indiana) So, I have some friends but am mostly alone except for my wife, kids and family. But what do you expect from an 18/19 year old point man who grew up but in some ways has always walked point throughout his life.

So ultimately, as I looked around and there was nothing left for me at work. I had little choice but to take early retirement at the age of 55. They didn't want leaders, they wanted followers. I have been a leader all my life, but it's all over and it's kind of sad. I always tried to do the right thing, and would do things others didn't want to do because someone had to do them. Some people ask me why I retired so early at the age of 55. I tell them the year in Vietnam counted for five to ten years—so it's not early. And I really believe that.

I went to one more 173d reunion and saw Smitty and his wife Tina a couple more times. But, I'm not sure if I will be going to anymore reunions. I looked through the names of those attending that last reunion—two or three times. And I finally realized that I was mostly looking for ghosts. I will stay in touch with Smitty and his wife Tina and see them when I can. But Ray and Mike were my best friends and they are dead. Vietnam and point killed Ray with 16 days left. After being told many times to speed up, Ray said F.... it—don't mean nothin and was killed. I know Mike was killed in a hang gliding accident. But make no mistake about it, Mike was killed by Vietnam. Mike was battling the same haunts and horrors from Vietnam that I face from time to time. I still have my 'back pocket' as frayed as it might be and my family. Mike coped by being an adrenaline junky. Its funny, but hang gliding is kind of like walking point—you are all alone and if there is no-one left to link-up, point wins and may God bless Mike's soul. And as for Smitty, point was telling him 'it don't mean nothing— you've got a million dollar wound' as Smitty was bleeding out, went into a coma and nearly died.

So somehow point always seems to win and point men tend to lose—sooner or later. Point was whispering 'don't mean nothin' to Ray, Mike and Smitty when it got them. And I know that little voice in my head is point that still reminds me from time to time that it 'don't mean nothin'. So for Ray, Mike,

Smitty, myself and for all the other point men who have been haunted by point's whispers—may God rest our souls..... .

THE END

AFTERWORD

Now I am 58 years old and was pretty much forced into early retirement from work. I am still married to Judy (38 years) who waited for me during Vietnam and has helped me through the aftermath with my PTSD. I have my health care through the VA in Minneapolis. It is a wonderful facility (not perfect but what hospital is) and I am very satisfied with my health care. I like being at the VA with veterans after spending my 30 year business career with so very few veterans. I decided to give something back by volunteering at the VA Medical Center 2 days a week. I enjoy the interactions I have with all the vets—from WWII to the current soldiers returning from Iraq and all those in between. I have met many Vietnam vets and some from my unit—the 173rd Airborne Brigade. Unfortunately I am seeing many of the Iraq vets going to the PTSD clinic at the medical center. But PTSD is a reality for many of the combatants in war and I am glad to see these warriors getting treatment and hope they will not have to battle PTSD for the rest of their lives. I feel good about anything I can do to help the vets at the medical center.

I also decided to get more and ongoing treatment for my PTSD. Although I was hesitant and concerned about counseling dredging up old memories, writing this book has done just that—but not in a bad or devastating way like I feared. So I am re-enrolled in the PTSD clinic at the V.A. and am seeing counselors who are very skilled at helping me understand my feelings and cope with my recurring PTSD symptoms.

Also, with my free time I am able to spend more time with my granddaughter, Maya. My daughter, Leslie, is a single mom. And Maya's dad is not involved at all. So I am the closest thing to a dad that Maya has. So it is good that I'm able to spend time and do things with Maya. I have coached her basketball team for the last two years (they call me 'grandpa coach'). In the summer I take her to baseball games and we hang out playing basketball and just goofing around. We also take her to a resort at Trout Lake where we fish, swim and have a glorious time.

I think these are the things I am meant to do at this time in my life. And **'they do mean something'**.

And I'll see Smitty from time to time. Maybe someday Smitty and I can talk about 'point whispers' but if the haunts are still there and it turns out we can't—**'it don't mean nothin'**..... .

As far as this book, I hope I have given the reader an insight into some of the nasty and brutal realities of war as well as the aftermath. Although wars can be won, the combatants seldom win—they always seem to lose one way or another.

GLOSSARY

AIT—advanced individual training which trains a soldier for their job in the Army

Cherry Jumps—these were the 5 static line parachute jumps that were made during jump week in jump school to earn your parachute wings. It was said these jumps 'broke your cherry'

CO—commanding officer. This referrers to the company commander of our infantry companies in the 173d. These officers were generally Captains who reported to the battalion commander

combat assault (C.A.)—is a combat assault using Huey helicopters. Each helicopter had a pilot, co-pilot and two door gunners with M60 machine guns on each of the two open sides. These Hueys had no doors so 4 to 6 of us could sit on the floor of the helicopter with our feet on the runners as we were flown to the landing zone (L.Z.) Prior to the our landing, Cobra gun ships (helicopters with miniguns and 40 millimeter cannons) would strafe the landing zone. If the gun ships received return fire it was a 'hot L.Z and we would receive word from the Huey crew that it was 'hot' and to be ready. If there was no return fire it was a cold L.Z

constatina wire—circular spools of barbed wire that are stretched and extended outside and around a perimeter. Normally the constatina wire would be about two to three feet in diameter and very difficult to get over or through. Often we would place trip flares in the constatina wire to detect attempts to cut the wire

DEROS—this was the date that each soldier in Vietnam was scheduled to return home. Normally this was one year from the day you got to Vietnam

DR—disciplinary report. This was the equivalent of a 'ticket' that was given by military police.

FNG—'f…. . new guys' a disparaging term for new guys who had just been sent out in the field and had not experienced combat

getting over—getting off easy. Usually referring to guys who were back in base camp either temporarily or with permanent assignments

houch—is a slang word for sleeping quarters. It can refer to the 'mini-tents' that we constructed out in the field from our ponchos—bracing them up with the small trees/sticks we would cut with our machetes.

Houch can also refer to grass huts that Vietnamese constructed for their homes in villages. And houch can also refer to tent-type barracks back in our fire support base or base camp.

Kit Carson Scouts—normally RVN soldiers but sometime Montagnards who were specially trained to walk point. Some American combat units periodically used them to assist in walking point

mortars/mortar rounds—these are small artillery rounds that are fired from a portable tube. These tubes and rounds are light enough for infantry type of units to carry them and use them in the field. These were used by all of the armed forces in Vietnam—American, NVA and Viet Cong

NVA—North Vietnamese Army. These were the regular Army forces from North Vietnam that infiltrated south into South Vietnam to engage American forces. They most often operated in the jungles and generally followed the Ho Chi Man trail through the cover of the jungle to South Vietnam. This trail was also used to transport supplies to the NVA forces in South Vietnam. The NVA used AK47 rifles and wore uniforms identifying them as NVA soldiers.

RTO—radio/telephone operator. Normally they carried a PRC-25 battery powered radio

ruck sack—like a very big back pack. They were nylon on an aluminum frame. Used by an infantry soldier to carry all of their food and gear

RVN's—South Vietnamese soldiers from the **R**epublic of **V**iet **N**am

satchel charges—these were explosives generally used by the Viet Cong. They were explosives and shrapnel that were placed in small suit cases like valises. These were used during ambushes or other close combat situations where they could be thrown at the enemy

stand down—term used for a rest period back in base camp. Usually it was for 5 or 7 days after spending 30 to 45 days out in the field

trip flares—these were small flares that had like a 'hair trigger' that was attached to very fine (almost invisible) wire. A trip flare would be set and then the wire would be stretched across an area that was vulnerable to enemy infiltration. Once set, the slightest movement against the wire would trigger the flare. The flare would not only warn us of advancing enemy but would also illuminate the immediate area so we could see what set it off

Viet Cong—these were South Vietnamese combatants (against American forces) who were said to be North Vietnamese sympathizers. The Viet Cong were in many South Vietnamese villages and were often recruited by the NVA using terroristic tactics. One such tactic was for the NVA to go into a South Vietnamese village, kill the village chief, cut his head off and put it on a spear in the middle of the village. Then they gathered the villagers and told all of the men that they would become Viet Cong or their heads would be on the spear. Such NVA recruiting tactics were very effective. The Viet Cong wore no uniforms and were impossible to identify from other South Vietnamese

978-0-595-47521-0
0-595-47521-3

CPSIA information can be obtained at www.ICGtesting.com
Printed in the USA
BVOW081538250213

314122BV00001B/98/A